The Ghost of Put-In-Bay

Daryl J. Lukas

ISBN (Print): 978-1-09838-123-3
ISBN (eBook): 978-1-09838-124-0

for Diane

"Show me a man with no vices
and I'll show you
a man with no virtues."

— ABRAHAM LINCOLN

Though not incorporated as a village until 1876, Put-In-Bay was actually given its name by the Great Lakes sailors of the 1700's. Situated within the northern coastline of South Bass Island, it naturally shelters and provides a safe harbor from most on-coming storms which typically travel along the path of the westerly winds. Hence, if it was feasible to do so, these men would often times "put-in" and wait for any hazardous conditions to pass.

1.

His last name was Stachowiak. (stuh-HO-vee-ack)

This was a fact which no one knew – at least, no one around here.

Everyone simply called him "Old Joe."

He'd been living here for about a month and was staying at a little motel off of Catawba Avenue in this picturesque village of Put-In-Bay, Ohio.

It's located on South Bass Island (in the southwestern part of Lake Erie) about twenty miles off the coast of Port Clinton and Old Joe had been in love with its summertime breezes and neon lights ever since he was twenty-one and had taken that ferry ride across for the first time.

Of course there'd been some changes through the years, especially since those mid-seventies, now with more boats and restaurants and people, but the quaint downtown still reminded him of a miniature toy city that he used to play on with his matchbox cars when he was a kid.

There was Frosty's, where he had performed his very first "beer-slide;" and the Beer Barrel Saloon, home of the world's longest bar; and The Roundhouse, where he and his buddies used to drink gallons of beer from those big red buckets and then go gallivanting around wearing the empties on their heads; and the famous Boathouse, where the legendary Pat Dailey would play his guitar and sing until the wee hours of the morning.

But on this night, as the sun began to set on another perfect June day, he was sitting at the bar at Mojito Bay and had gone away from his customary Coors Light – of which he would usually drink at least a case on any given day – and was enjoying a rather delicious concoction called a "Hurricane" instead; made with one part light rum, one part dark rum, one-half part over-proofed rum, passion fruit syrup, and lemon juice. But Old Joe didn't care about any of that. All he knew was that it tasted "damn good."

And this delightful "change-of-pace" had come by way of a bartender named Diago (dee-AH-go) – pronounced with a softer-sounding "ah" rather than the stronger "ay" that one would typically hear when saying the words "San Diego" for example – and it was this type of distinction that was important to Old Joe. He'd been a public school teacher for some 32 years and had always made it a special point to learn not only a person's name but to also know the correct spelling and proper enunciation. And, in many ways, this was the very essence of the man, for at the core of his being were some wonderful traits – such as his intelligence and sense of humor, along with his sense of decency and fair play.

However, he was also a drunk.

Now exactly how this had happened, or why, wasn't clear. Only that on his long journey back to the island, during those intermittent times when he'd been away, it seemed that life hadn't turned out the way he'd planned. Maybe something unfortunate had taken place, or perhaps it was simply a matter of fate, but Old Joe had never married and didn't have any children that he knew of so, with the exception of a younger brother (whom he hadn't seen in years) and a couple of distant friends, he was alone in this world. And as some of the locals would later suggest, this fact by itself may've been the reason for his drinking.

Though, whatever the cause, the result was evident – he had changed.

He was no longer the casual drinker or the weekend binger, rather he was now a full-blown alcoholic and what some employees around the island had come to refer to as "damaged goods."

Because, within the next hour or two, or most certainly by the next day, those names over which Old Joe would make such a fuss would escape him. Then the entire exercise would have to begin again. And then again. Thus, after only four weeks on the island, all of the bartenders were well aware of Old Joe – and for many he had already become a moot point.

However, while some took offense to his constant drunkenness, others did not and – though it seemed somewhat funny at the time, if not ironic – Old Joe began to use this same criteria when making his own personal list of the island's bartenders and separating them into two distinct categories.

If, for example, you had at one time or another turned your back on him or simply walked away, because you'd had enough of Old Joe's routine and couldn't take it anymore, then you most assuredly would've gone down in his mental gradebook as "one of the bad ones." On the other hand, if you didn't seem to mind his incessant forgetfulness, or his unpredictable mood swings or sometimes foul behavior, then you would've been sure to receive a check mark in the column headed, "The Good Ones."

Diago was most definitely in this latter group.

For no matter how many times in the past Old Joe had forgotten his name, and had then subjected him to that same drill of spelling and enunciation, Diago would simply smile and play along. Furthermore, in Old Joe's more lucid moments, Diago had even gone so far as to entrust him with some quite personal information. Like the fact that he had come from Guatemala. That he had worked on a banana farm from the age of six. That he'd never known his father. That his mother had died when he was ten. That he'd come to the United States with his uncle. That he considered his uncle to be a great man.

And Old Joe would try his best to remember these things because, somewhere along the way, Diago had become his friend.

As evidenced once more on this night – with the outdoor area at Mojito's getting crowded and with Diago in the midst of serving other customers – when the affable young employee still found time to yell across the bar, "Hey old man, you want another Hurricane, or are we back to Coors Light?"

Old Joe loved the attention – he reveled in it.

"Nah," he shouted back, "neither." Then after a brief pause he said, "You put me in the mood for somethin' different – whatcha got?"

"Oh, really now," exclaimed Diago. "Wow, what's this?"

4

"Ok," he continued, and while wiping his hands with a bar rag he walked up a little closer to his new buddy and asked, "how 'bout a Bahama Mama?"

The old man let out a laugh. He liked it instantly.

"Hell yeah," he said. "What's in it?"

"It's another rum drink," replied Diago, "with some pineapple and a few other things."

"All right," said Old Joe, "sounds good."

So for the next few minutes he sat there by himself quietly sipping on his reddish-orange drink with the funny name. Then, after paying his bill, he got up from his barstool, slipped an extra twenty underneath his empty glass, and went on his way.

It was sometime around midnight.

It was some weekday in June.

But as he walked southward down Catawba Avenue, he knew for certain that it was a beautiful evening, that he was in the great state of Ohio in the year of Our Lord 2018, that Donald J. Trump was President of the United States, and that one month earlier he, Joseph Stachowiak, had somehow become sixty-seven years old.

Then he stopped for a moment.

"Sixty-seven," he thought, *"holy shit."*

2.

For perhaps the first time in his life, Old Joe wasn't worried about money.

If truth be told, he wasn't concerned in the least.

He'd cashed-out his savings and paid-off his debts and – after partying for a solid month – still had seventy-five grand.

"Just as long as I can make it to Labor Day," he thought.

A couple hundred or so had been left in the bank from some old "rainy day" fund, but most of his money was now hidden above a ceiling tile in the corner of his bathroom. He kept it in an old gray gym bag (the kind with a zipper) that he would take down each morning to supply himself with the funds that were required to make it through the day. He was staying at a place close to the downtown bars called "Victoria Station" (which cost him one hundred-fifty a night) and along with his daily spending habits of anywhere from about two to three-fifty meant that he was giving himself a per diem of roughly five hundred dollars.

Of course there were always going to be those miscellaneous expenditures for gambling or gratuities or what have you – like buying a few drinks for any friendly acquaintances he'd happen to meet along the way – but he'd done the math and taken everything into account and so far things were looking good.

So Old Joe had other things on his mind that night as he left Mojito Bay and stopped in at Hooligan's Irish Pub.

Now this wasn't normally one of his late-night haunts, though it had nothing to do with the establishment or its employees, it's just that his stomach had been giving him some trouble these days and those heavy dark malts were no longer ideal.

But tonight, for one reason or another, an Irish ale was sounding just right and as things turned out he was in luck – because a corner barstool was open.

"Hallelujah," he thought, "maybe somebody up there likes me after all."

Of all the things in this world that Old Joe considered to be holy and sacred, a corner barstool was near the top of the list – and there it was.

No matter the place, Old Joe liked to sit at the bar. That was a given.

In fact, for him, it was usually a barstool or he was out the door. However, as with most things in life, there were a few exceptions to this rule – namely, The Roundhouse and The Boathouse. On any given night chances were pretty slim that he was going to find a seat at either one of those bars so, at times, he simply had to make due.

Though, for now, he was at Hooligan's and had just laid claim to that most prized possession – his pinnacle of existence.

He ordered a tall glass of Murphy's Irish Red and sat there quietly, by himself, as was often the case, pondering some of life's more mysterious questions. Old Joe liked to think – and he thought about a lot of things. Besides drinking, it was his favorite pastime.

Like tonight, for instance, when he began thinking about why his lager was tasting so good. Was it because of the fruit that Diago had put in his earlier drinks? Could that *still* be affecting his taste? Well, whatever it was, Old Joe was liking the result for his ale had a refreshing citrusy taste – though, he was still somewhat leery, for he had long been a proponent of trying to avoid things that he deemed to be "too healthy" for his system.

Then he thought about how he'd gotten here – not to this barstool, exactly, but rather to this particular point in his life. How his once strong and virile body had become this busted-up and broken-down shell. He thought about his days of playing high school football, how he used to explode through the four hole between guard and tackle and how the local newspaper used to print that he could *"run like the wind"* while starring at halfback for St. Ignatius.

He thought about his dead parents and some of his dead friends and of his only brother, the one whom he hadn't seen or spoken to in years, and about that saying of how *"the good die young"* and why no one had found a cure for cancer.

His father had died of cancer – pancreatic.

And as Old Joe sat there he found it hard to believe that it had been over twenty years since he'd watched his old man pass away.

"Inoperable," the doctors said.

"Fucking assholes," he thought.

He remembered those final agonizing days and the bewildered look on his father's face as the drugs that the doctor had prescribed quickly robbed him of his senses.

And he wondered if it had all been just a ploy, perhaps some sleazy "cost-cutting" measure with what he now knew about doctors and insurance companies and the like.

"Fucking assholes," he thought again.

Then he thought about the women that he'd known in his life and if any still thought about him, then he looked at the empty barstool that was sitting next to his and took the final swigs of his beer.

He was starting to get tired and a little bit sappy as the synapses in his brain began to misfire. He knew this was the case because he actually loved his life – and always had – with all of the drinking and carousing and gambling.

But, for Old Joe, there was the rub.

For though he liked to drink, he was still a proud man who didn't like to embarrass himself by slurring his words or stumbling down the sidewalk or by doing any of those other things that naturally came with being a drunk. Even at that moment, he was beginning to nod off right there at the bar.

So, after deciding to leave, he pulled out a twenty and quietly slipped it underneath his glass. Then he got up from his barstool and proceeded toward the door. He tried his best to maintain a straight line.

He left without incident.

3.

A few soft streaks of sunlight came filtering through the blinds as Old Joe was lying motionless on his bed. He could feel the warmth of his blood as it went coursing rhythmically through his veins, as it pounded at his temples, and on the inside of his head.

It hurt to think.

It hurt to breathe.

It hurt, at this point, to be alive.

But then, it was always painful that next day – having to start again.

The initial opening of the eyes, the coughing, the hacking, the swinging of his legs out of bed.

The washing down of meds with last night's warm beer.

The Viagra, the Valsartan, the Vicodin.

The steroids, the hormones, the hydrochlorothiazide.

The Motrin, the Excedrin, and so forth.

And all of this before his morning constitutional, or what he referred to as "the three kings" – his shit, shower and shave (with the shave being optional.)

This was Old Joe's routine. No matter how much he had to drink the night before, or how hard his head was pounding, he would always try to get to the bars before 10 – usually the Beer Barrel – to feel the best breezes and to nab the best barstool.

After his shower, he'd go to the fridge to ponder his meager choices.

Today's menu was standard fare – a few slices of bologna, some left over pizza, pickles, olives, and mustard.

So, per usual, he decided to forgo whatever delicacies there were and simply grabbed a cold beer to help him get dressed. Then, along with a cream-colored pair of cargo shorts and an old pale-blue Detroit Tigers T-shirt, he put on his "Papa Lou's" ball cap and was ready to go. He filled his wallet with cash, slapped on an extra splash of Brut aftershave, and then headed out the door to greet the day.

It was another beautiful June morning.

4.

When Old Joe walked into the Beer Barrel Saloon it was a half-past nine. He liked it there, especially when it was empty, so it was usually his first stop of the day.

And why wouldn't he like it? Old Joe was a bar connoisseur and the Beer Barrel had the longest bar in the world. That's right – in the entire world. It measured 405 feet and 10 inches long and was shaped something like a rectangle, a very strange rectangle, with a lot of juts and nooks and crannies. Which meant that, in theory, it was the easiest place in the world to find a corner barstool – so in the eyes of Old Joe it was like heaven itself.

The Beer Barrel was known for its nightly entertainment and it had always mystified the old man as to how such a large and lively place, filled with hundreds of fun-loving people, could be so peaceful just a few hours later.

But this is when he liked it the most, when hardly anyone else was there – just him, a couple of bartenders, and a seagull or two – with that incredible breeze coming in from straight off the lake.

Though it was more than that, for Old Joe had always taken pleasure in admiring those simple things in life that most others did not. To him, there was a certain kind of hidden beauty in almost everything – in all sorts of people and places and things – you only needed to look.

So that's why he would always make the effort of going to the Beer Barrel in the morning, because no one else would be there to witness what he saw.

But first things first – he needed a drink. Well, actually, he would order a combination of drinks, a hangover remedy that he'd perfected through the years – a Bloody Mary, a Coors Light, a Diet Coke, and a water – all at the same time.

Then, with masterful precision, like a surgeon bringing a patient back to life, Old Joe would alternate his sips until his eyes began to truly open for the first time and he could see the world again.

And then he would get on with his morning. Looking out at the lake, feeling those incredible breezes, smelling that fresh air. Sometimes he'd read a book, or write a few things down in his journal, or study the latest "lines" in the sports section. But mostly, he'd just sit there and think – or talk to Eddie.

He was the morning bartender at the Beer Barrel.

Eddie was a mature young man with a calm demeanor who went by various nicknames including "Eddie B.," "Fast Eddie," and occasionally "Ringo." Now the morning hours were usually when Old Joe was at his best and he could remember a few things, but he would be damned if he could ever tell you Eddie's last name – even though he knew that it started with a "B" and had been told to him by Eddie himself on more than one occasion. So, in Old Joe's mind, the "B" simply stood for bartender. And as for "Fast Eddie" and "Ringo?" Well, it probably had something to do with the fact that Eddie was a pretty good-looking kid and did fairly well with the ladies. Although, unlike most guys his age, you never heard him bragging about any of his sexual conquests – at least he had never done so in front of Old Joe – and that was one of the things that had endeared him to the old man.

He stood about six feet tall with an athletic build. He had thick, dark hair and a pleasant smile. But as far as Old Joe was concerned, the "Fast Eddie" name came from his work behind the bar.

Eddie was an excellent bartender. He always kept himself busy and made one of the best damned Bloody Marys that Old Joe had ever tasted. He was polite, a good conversationalist, and just an all-around nice guy who was saving-up to pay his way through college.

But the main reason why Old Joe thought that Eddie was such a fine bartender, was the fact that he wasn't a "globber." In other words, he would never try to "glob" all over you and blow smoke up your ass to work the tip. Yet, he was always within earshot so you never had to go looking for him if you needed a beer.

And since the old man had never been one to be easily impressed, I think it's fair to say that the young bartender had won him over.

Yes, Old Joe liked "Eddie B."

5.

Meet Sal.

Like Eddie, he worked at the Beer Barrel – though not as a bartender.

He was a bouncer. And more importantly, he was good with numbers.

In other words, Sal was Old Joe's bookie.

And with a name like Sal, you might be imagining some Italian guy dressed in a matching suit with a pair of shiny black shoes and with some loose connection to the mob. But, no. Sorry to disappoint.

Rather, Sal was a Samoan. And he was a big dude.

I mean, this was one large human being – about the size of a small steer. Or, picture if you will a standard-sized industrial refrigerator, only with some enormous arms and legs and with one "big ass" head sitting up on top – and an ugly one at that – with mutton chops. That was Sal.

And though Sal was one mean-looking son of a bitch, he was actually a pretty sweet guy. Oh sure, if you crossed him, or if you couldn't pay your debt, he might still bust your arm or maybe break a finger or two, but he would do it in a nice way. Simply put, he'd chosen a very suitable career.

It all started rather innocently one day while Old Joe was sitting at the bar. He'd overheard "Big Sal" talking on the phone with one of his boys in Vegas and one thing led to another, as they usually do, and before you knew it – voila! Sal was Old Joe's bookie.

Now it's no secret that Old Joe liked to gamble.

After all, it was fun and exciting and, generally speaking, was a good way to pass the time. However, more than anything else, Old Joe liked to win. But even when he lost, which was probably more times than not these days, he really wasn't that upset

That's because he knew that Sal needed the money.

Now you may be asking, *"Why would a gambler care whether or not his bookie needed money?"*

Good question.

Well, first of all, the money wasn't really all that important to Old Joe. And secondly, and more importantly, was the fact that his heart truly went out to "Big Sal."

You see, along with everything else that was going on in Sal's active and sometimes sordid life, he had a disabled sister who he always tried to help out as best he could.

And this wasn't one of those sob stories created by some of the locals in their spare time either – it was the real deal.

Sal and his sister had been witnessed off the island at various times with the big man attending to her and pushing her wheel chair.

However, verification wasn't necessary, because the old man could smell bullshit comin' from a mile away. Furthermore, Sal had never brought up his sister's disability in conversation, not once – and he respected that.

So, I guess you could say that in Old Joe's book, "Big Sal" was ok.

6.

Old Joe liked pretty things.

He appreciated beauty.

And the wonderful thing about Old Joe was, he could find it in almost anything.

He could find it in a brick, or in a bottle cap, or in a blade of grass.

He could find it in a hamburger, or in a cigar, or in an ice cold beer.

However, on this particular day, while having a beer at Frosty's, a great little bar and restaurant renowned for their pizza, Old Joe was finding beauty in the shape of a young brunette.

A tall, slender, rather leggy young brunette. She was wearing a white cotton top that was tied at the midriff and a pair of cut-off blue jeans with those frayed white threads that accentuated her tanned thighs and … ok, wait a minute. I know what you're thinking. You're starting to think poorly of Old Joe – aren't you? You're beginning to form an opinion.

Well, before we go any further, perhaps I should give you *my* opinion.

Old Joe was a good guy.

He was a decent and honest man.

He'd tell ya' where you stood – period.

Now, yes, he was a drunk. And at times he had a foul mouth – granted. There's no denying that the man had his share of problems.

But, even though he was by no means a saint, he wasn't a horrible person either. He wasn't a terrorist, or a racist, or an ageist. In fact, he wasn't any kind of an *"ist"* at all. He wasn't a narcissist, or a pedofile, or a homophobe. He didn't have any delusions of grandeur, or pent-up hostilities, or perverted fantasies. And, perhaps above all else, he was not a sexist.

Old Joe loved women – he truly did.

He saw them as equals and treated them well. And though he was no longer in his twenties or thirties – or even in his fifties for that matter – he was still a man who he enjoyed looking at beautiful women.

Is that so wrong?

Does that make him a bad egg?

Seriously, in the long and short of things, where does a person like Old Joe measure on the scale?

Well, I've said enough.

You decide.

7.

Now, where were we? Ah, yes, Frosty's Bar.

And Old Joe was looking at a young brunette.

So, let's continue.

She was standing at the bar and he was looking at her deep tan, and her perfect skin, and at just that hint of cleavage peeking through her unbuttoned blouse, and at her thin little waist and her firm thighs, and at those tight cut-off shorts with a tiny rip in the back pocket that was ... ok, once again, let's pause here for a moment.

I'm sorry, but it appears as if Old Joe was staring – right?

Like I explained, the man was no saint.

However, there was no malicious intent with his actions either. I know this because Old Joe had never intentionally meant to hurt anyone in his life. He was simply trying to enjoy the beautiful scenery.

Though, unfortunately, the young woman's boyfriend didn't quite see it that way and decided to give Old Joe a piece of his mind.

"Hey old man," he said, "why don't you try putting those eye-balls back in their sockets?"

"Oh, sorry young fella," answered a sheepish Old Joe, "didn't mean any harm."

"Yeah, I'll bet," said the boyfriend, "why don't you go fuck yourself?"

Old Joe didn't respond. He thought it best to just leave things the way they were. You see, to him, the world was indeed an incredible place filled with amazing beauty – and if he wanted to stare at a spectacular sunset, or at a remarkable painting, or at a pretty young woman then, by God, he was going to do so.

And he didn't think that he owed anyone an explanation.

If others were to somehow misinterpret his actions, or think poorly of him for whatever reason, he simply didn't care. As he saw it, that was one of the blessings of getting old.

Because, deep down, even with all of his problems and misgivings, Old Joe still believed that he was a good person.

He simply walked to the beat of his own drum – that's all.

With him, there were no dark, covert mysteries or even a "gray area." Everything was out in the open and pretty much "black and white."

Once, while making a toast to a friend who was going through a divorce, he said, "Here's to broken promises – that good intentions will eventually count for somethin.'"

That was Old Joe.

8.

Believe it or not, every now and then Old Joe liked to take a walk in the park. However, that was mostly because of where Perry Park was located at Put-In-Bay – directly across from Delaware Avenue and smack dab in the middle of the downtown bars.

So sometimes, when leaving the Beer Barrel, instead of simply walking a little ways down the street to go to Frosty's, he would cross the street and walk into the park and do almost a complete circle before finally ending up there.

Perhaps if we make a map it will be easier for you to follow. So take out your imaginary pencil and begin to draw in your mind a rectangle, with the longest lines being on the top and bottom. Now, divide that rectangle into four equal quadrants by drawing two straight lines that bisect the opposing sides – and you already have the general layout of Perry Park at Put-In-Bay; with the right top and bottom boxes being the northeast and southeast quadrants, respectively, and with the left top and bottom boxes being the north-west and southwest quadrants. And now we'll simply add the names of the streets, with Bayview running east to west along the top (or north), with Hartford running north to south along the right side (or east), with Delaware running east to west along the bottom (or south) and with Catawba running north to south along the left side (or west.) And there you have it.

So now that we're finished, let's go for a walk. Pretend that it's a hot day and that you're at The Keys restaurant having a delicious cheeseburger and a beer. You would be nearest to the northeast quadrant by the intersection of Bayview and Hartford. And now let's say, for the sake of argument, that you wanted to head on over to the Beer Barrel, which is nearest to the southwest quadrant at the intersection of Delaware and Catawba. Well, you could simply walk along the sidewalks and experience for yourself all of the amazing shops and taverns, which is naturally what most of the first-timers do, or you could take a shortcut and walk through the park and feel the coolness of the shade underneath the large trees. Or, let's say that you were at The Boardwalk, which is at the intersection of Catawba and Bayview nearest to the northwest quadrant and you wanted to walk over to The Roundhouse, which is nearest to the southeast quadrant on Delaware. Once again, you could take the long way around or simply take a short cut through this magnificent little park.

And every so often that's where Old Joe would walk when making his way from the Beer Barrel to Frosty's. Like he was this morning, only Old Joe had now stopped his little journey and was standing in the park thinking about this most recent phenomenon he'd been witnessing. While walking through the park (or anywhere for that matter) he'd noticed that most of the people were looking at their cell phones and were oblivious to everything around them – and he found this new "shared trait" to be both abhorrent and most difficult to understand.

After all, here they were at Put-In-Bay, Ohio – at one of the most spectacular places on planet earth on yet another glorious June afternoon – and instead of looking around at the natural beauty and taking in all of God's incredible blessings, these idiots were staring at their phones.

And he wondered, *"What in the world could be so important?"*

But, after standing there for a moment, and then letting that question run through his mind for a while, he came to the conclusion that there was no good answer and decided to let it go and to move on.

Besides, he needed a beer.

So he left the park, crossing back over Delaware Avenue, and went to Frosty's.

9.

This was the day.

Old Joe was running "the circuit."

And by running, I actually mean walking, and sitting, and drinking, in a number of local establishments.

Because, to Old Joe, "the circuit" didn't include any of those outlying wineries that you had to get to by way of a golf cart, or any of those "stupid ass" swim-up bars that had become so prevalent in recent years, the ones that had changed the face of the island along with their accompanying hotels. Nope, not a chance. For when it came to "the circuit," or when it came to most things, Old Joe was (for lack of a better term) "old school."

To him, "the circuit" (or "the loop" as it was also known) still meant *only* the downtown bars off of the main avenues – from Delaware, to Hartford, to Bayview to Catawba – starting from any point and going in either direction; and having at least one drink at each location.

However, it wasn't going to be exactly like it had been in the old days.

That is, he wasn't going to be slamming shots and throwing down mixed drinks at every stop – only beer. Because, to be honest, the only reason that Old Joe had decided to do "the circuit" in the first place was to see if he still could. So, even though he wasn't going to do anything "crazy," like those old-time "boilermakers" for instance – when he would drop a shot glass of whiskey into his mug of draft beer and then guzzle them both simultaneously – he was going to try to hit all of the downtown bars on his list.

Now, on a typical day, Old Joe's schedule went something like this:

The Beer Barrel 9:30 – 12:00
Frosty's Bar 12:00 – 3:00
The Roundhouse 3:00 – 6:00
The Boathouse 6:00 – 10:00
Mojito Bay 10:00 – ?
(These hours, of course, were subject to change.)

So, like usual, he planned to start at the Beer Barrel and then head east toward Hartford Avenue. And he also thought that it would be a good idea to still end the day as he always did with the friendly face of Diago at Mojito Bay.

Although, in order to run "the circuit," he had to make some changes to the middle of his day; thus, Old Joe's pilgrimage transpired as follows:

He began at the Beer Barrel and then proceeded to Frosty's. From there, he went to The Roundhouse (which didn't open 'til noon), then to T&J's, then to the Boathouse, then to The Keys (after which he took a well-deserved 45 minute interlude for a little siesta in the park), then to The Boardwalk, then to Topsy Turvey's (and by this point he was really starting to feel it) and then to Mossbacks and finally, Mojito Bay.

And needless to say, by the time our warrior-hero had made it all the way around to see his friend Diago, he was really in no condition to do much of anything (though that still didn't stop him from sitting down and having a few more beers.) However, due to his advanced planning, Diago was there to keep a close eye on the old man and tried his best to protect him from any additional harm or embarrassment. And then, at long last, he was able to coax him into a taxi for the short ride back to his motel room.

But none of that really mattered to Old Joe.

Because, when it was over, and for the rest of his life, all he would remember about that day was … *"I did it!"*

And so he had.

One more time.

10.

It was half-past eleven on a drizzly Sunday morning and Old Joe was still in bed. His head was pounding. He felt awful. Even worse than usual, if that's possible.

He tried rolling over a couple of times to try and make himself more comfortable, but eventually said, "Fuck it."

So he got up and took his meds, then after going to the john he removed a ceiling tile from the bathroom to retrieve his old gym bag where he kept his money.

He'd been gambling a little more than usual lately – and losing.

That's the thing about gambling.

So he wanted to see how much he had left. It was only mid-June and he discovered that he was already down to just under sixty-five grand. It didn't take a mathematician to figure out that at this rate (with his five hundred dollar a day allowance – including his one hundred-fifty dollar a night rent) he was going to have to cool it just a bit if he wanted to make it to Labor Day, which had been his plan all along.

"If it was only football season," he thought. Old Joe had a lot more confidence betting on both college and pro football than he did on baseball or, heaven forbid, golf. But, nevertheless, he had some money on a couple of games that afternoon, so he grabbed the TV remote to check the listings.

It was almost noon.

He flipped through the stations until he eventually came upon a program called "Mass for Shut-Ins." Then, surprising even himself, he sat down on the edge of the bed and began to watch.

It was the first time that he'd gone to church in years.

11.

Old Joe went for a walk this morning.

Not to a bar, but to a monument – which for him was usually the same thing. However, in this case, he went to Perry's Victory and International Peace Memorial. It's about a half-mile or so up the road from the downtown bars and towers over the northeastern part of South Bass Island.

At 352 feet, it's the world's most massive Doric column.

Although, no matter how impressive this monument might be, you're probably thinking that it was strange for Old Joe to have not been at a bar; and, quite frankly, it was. But being a former history teacher, he'd always been fascinated by the amazing story of Commodore Oliver Hazard Perry. Besides, he was only planning on staying for an hour or so and he took along a flask filled with some Southern Comfort for the trip.

The story behind the monument goes something like this:

During the War of 1812, when Great Britain had the greatest navy in the world and the American Navy was nothing more than a rag-tag gathering of some ill-equipped ships, like a flotilla from "The Island of Misfit Toys," Commodore Perry – almost single-handedly – defeated the British in the Battle of Lake Erie off the coast of South Bass Island.

A few weeks earlier, his good friend James Lawrence, captain of the ill-fated *Chesapeake,* had been killed in action with his dying words, "Don't give up the ship." Commodore Perry was so moved by his friend's heroism, that not only did he name his own flagship the *Lawrence,* but he had a sailmaker embroider a personal "motto flag" with those same incredible dying words. Then, during the battle, while being out-numbered six ships to one, and after having lost nearly all of his men on the burning *Lawrence,* Commodore Perry ordered his battle flag taken down. Through the smoke, the British were watching and began to cheer as Perry boarded a gig with four oarsmen and began to pull away from the doomed ship.

They fully expected that he would surrender his sword.

Though after having momentarily disappeared from their view, Perry miraculously reappeared on his sister ship the *Niagara;* however, when he lowered the battle flag on that ship as well, the British began to cheer once more, believing that they had finally won.

But then quickly up the mast went his motto flag with the words, "Don't give up the ship," and as the stunned British looked on, Perry laid down all sail and attacked.

What happened after that took only fifteen minutes, and when it was over he sent the following message ashore:

"We have met the enemy and they are ours; two ships, two brigs, one schooner, and one sloop. Yours with great respect and esteem, O.H. Perry."

So that's why Old Joe went for a walk.

12.

You'll never guess who Old Joe ran into on his way back from the Perry Memorial – none other than his old friend, Walter the dog.

Walter was a Jack Russell Terrier that would come into Frosty's from time to time. He was white and brown and cute as hell, and the old man liked him a lot. Although, he wasn't quite sure who his owners were since he'd seen him with a number of different people. There was an older guy who sat at the bar (Old Joe couldn't remember his name) and a young girl who'd come in a couple of times to order a pizza, along with another fella, maybe her boyfriend. But, it didn't matter.

Old Joe loved dogs and he'd owned a few himself over the years.

There was Sam, a mutt; Sinji, a white Lhasa Apso; Bogey, a classic Jack Russell; and Charlie, a black and white Malshi. They were all good dogs. Then again, according to him, it was hard to find a bad one – he pretty much thought that every dog was a good one.

And so, there was Old Joe walking down Delaware Avenue heading back to either Frosty's or the Beer Barrel, he hadn't quite made up his mind, when he went past the Chicken Patio and caught a whiff of that fresh poultry on the grill. The chicken there had always been incredible and back in the day Old Joe could really eat. I mean, sometimes he'd shovel food in his mouth so fast that you'd be afraid he might lose a finger. Though, since having become a drunk, like he was, food was seen more as mere sustenance – but, boy oh boy, that chicken smelled amazing.

And that was all that was needed these days for him to change plans, to change direction in midstream – so he thought, *"You know what? I'm gonna have myself some chicken!"* Along with corn on the cob, a freshly-buttered roll, and a cold bottle of Coors Light. Then as he was sitting there, thinking that this morning couldn't get much better, he felt Walter pawing at his leg. He'd come out of nowhere.

Old Joe looked around to see if he could find one of his owners, but there was just Walter, looking back up at him with those big brown eyes of his. So he pulled off a couple pieces of chicken and fed them to his friend. Then he gave him a couple more, along with a sip of his beer.

And there they were on that beautiful June morning, just two old buddies sharing a meal.

13.

Old Joe had cancer.

It had been discovered some ten years earlier.

But what he remembered most about that day, other than the doctor telling him the bad news, were these two red balloons that had gone skipping across the parking lot just before he'd entered the building. *"How odd,"* he thought, because balloons were supposed to just take off and go soaring high into the air, like Superman with his red cape.

Though, looking back, he now thought that those balloons had been some kind of an omen. Because, as it turned out, it was his prostate.

This is what flashed through Old Joe's mind as he was listening to a band blaring away at The Boathouse. It was a Saturday night and he was getting drunk with Maddie from Cincinnati. Seriously. That's how she'd introduced herself only a couple hours before. She just walked up to Old Joe and said, "Hi, I'm Maddie from Cincinnati."

No shit! And let me tell ya', he was more than happy to make her acquaintance.

She was somewhere in her mid-fifties, but she still had all of those marvelous curves in all of the right places and you could pretty much tell that back in the day she used to really be somethin'.

"And even now," thought Old Joe, Maddie from Cincinnati was a very attractive woman. She was wearing a baseball cap with her pony tail coming out of the back which had always driven Old Joe wild. *"How fucking adorable,"* he thought. The cap was red, of course, for the Cincinnati Reds, and had the white "C" stitched in front.

They made nice conversation right from the start with none of those awkward pauses, and she even laughed at a few of his jokes which told Old Joe everything he needed to know. Then, after an hour or two, having already shared each other's stories and with the formalities aside, they both pretended as if they could no longer hear very well because of the band, which gave them a much needed break. After all, they weren't kids anymore and each one knew where this was going.

So they ended up getting good and plastered before deciding to leave and heading back to Old Joe's room. But, as they were crossing Hartford Avenue and he began making his way along with Maddie from Cincinnati and her red baseball cap, those damned balloons went racing through his mind again and he thought, *"I sure hope that I can get it up."*

14.

Each day, sometime in the middle of the afternoon, Old Joe would head over to The Roundhouse. He loved that bar. He couldn't get enough. To him, there was no better bar on the planet – period. That's because, when it's right, and I mean when the place is *really* jumpin'*, there's simply no other bar like it in the world.

It's an actual *round house,* built in 1873, with a natural wood floor and one kick-ass looking bar situated directly beneath and around the stage where some of the best local (and national) acts appear. There's this one guy who's played there for years named Mike "Mad Dog" Adams who Old Joe remembered from back in the eight-ies. Not only is he one helluva good musician, but he'll make you piss your pants from laughing so hard. However, fair warning, if you're easily offended you'd best stay clear, because nothing is off limits with this guy – nothing is sacred. And they still serve actual buckets of beer at The Roundhouse. Not like the kind that you're used to seeing at other bars, where they give you a bucket of ice with four bottles of beer for ten bucks or whatever; rather, your entire bucket is filled to the brim with draft beer from which you can typically draw about 12 cups – and you need a deft hand along with a lot practice in order to not spill at least a couple of those cups on the way back to your table. Back in the day, when Old Joe was in his early twenties, he and his friends used to drink from those red buckets until they were empty and then they'd walk around for the rest of the afternoon wearing the damned things on their heads – they were called "bucket heads" naturally – it was a different time.

And there used to be so much beer spilled on the floor that they would have to temporarily close the place down every couple of hours to hose down the *inside* of the bar – which they still did, of course, though not nearly as often. Then, when everyone was allowed back in, the whole place would be soaked – the wood floors, the picnic tables, the barstools, and anything that you may have left behind – but everything would smell so clean and fresh and you'd be chomping at the bit to restart the party.

Old Joe was kinda sweet on a couple of gals over there named Sherri and Becky. Old Joe had cute nicknames for each of them – "Sherri darlin'" and "little Becky" – they were both really fun girls with great personalities. But, that's just how The Roundhouse was – fun! Fun with a capital "F." In fact, Old Joe used to love that bar so much that, if he couldn't get a barstool, he would actually stand all afternoon.

And he always had a great time.

15.

As much as Old Joe loved The Roundhouse, he held a special place in his heart for The Boathouse. He usually went there in the evenings to drink some beer and to look at the pretty women and to generally soak up the atmosphere. But lately, he'd also been going there to see Sarita, a twenty-something waitress from Johannesburg. She was, quite honestly, one of the nicest people he'd ever met and was quickly becoming one of his "all-time" favorites.

And just like with The Roundhouse, this bar was one of those exceptions where Old Joe wouldn't mind the fact that he had to stand because you could rarely find a barstool; that is, unless you got there early in the afternoon when he was still busy visiting his other bars. However, recently he'd been sitting on a wooden bench against the front wall that seemed comfortable enough and was usually left wide open.

But, regardless of any seating issues, he always loved going there.

Especially when Pat Dailey was in town. He was a well-traveled musician who became a Great Lakes legend during the eighties and was an absolute fixture at Put-In-Bay. Then, after playing for years to standing room only crowds at the rowdy Beer Barrel, Dailey moved over to The Boathouse in '07 to give his songs a more intimate setting. He's written and performed dozens of classics that include the following:

the Great Lakes Song
Doobie and a Brew
Get Your Ass to Cleveland
I Ain't Drunk, I Just Been Drinkin'
(and of course,) the Put in Bay song.

For Old Joe, there were few things in life that were as special as listening to Pat Dailey sing the Put in Bay song at Put-In-Bay – but it was even more so when he was at The Boathouse. Perhaps because, by then, Dailey was getting up there in years and both men knew that the good times wouldn't last forever.

One night, however, years earlier, when Old Joe was still in his twenties and Pat Dailey was still playing at the Beer Barrel, the young man's love for The Boathouse created a small problem. He was there, once again, listening to the music while drinking and flirting and carrying on, but the last ferry off the island was leaving at 11:00 and when he looked at his watch it was 10:45.

And back then there were far fewer cottages on the island and only one major downtown hotel, so finding a place to stay for the night could at times be a little tricky.

Though being young and full of confidence he thought, *"No problem – I'll just hook-up with one of these pretty young ladies and spend the night on a boat or whatever.*" Well, as you may have guessed, Old Joe missed the ferry and closed down The Boathouse.

However, as luck would have it – *bad* luck that is – he didn't score with any of the women that night and the village police tended to frown on those vacationing drunkards with no place to go at 2:30 in the morning. In fact, they frowned so much that they would throw your ass in the "hoosegow" if they even caught a glimpse of you after three.

Now, there was only one ferry service back then as well (prior to the Jet Express days) and their depot was toward the most south-eastern part of the island roughly two miles from downtown. But since Old Joe didn't want to get busted by the cops, it seemed at that point to be his best option. So, somewhere around three in the morning, he started that long walk back toward the depot, hiding in the trees whenever a police car would cruise past. And then, upon finally reaching his destination, which was really nothing more than a glorified lean-to, he spent the next four hours or so lying on an old wooden bench and staring up at a Hoot Owl while trying to get some sleep.

But, Old Joe didn't hold any grudges.

All these years later, he still loved The Boathouse.

16.

It was 73 degrees at a quarter 'til noon on another sunny and breezy June day, and as Old Joe was walking down Delaware Avenue he spotted a man in a gray baseball cap looking his way. He was leaning against Frosty's while smoking a cigarette with one foot on the sidewalk and the other resting upon the brick wall, and as Old Joe got a little closer the man shouted "O-H" to which he responded "I-O."

It's the universal greeting for all Buckeyes, especially here at Put-In-Bay, and since Old Joe just happened to be wearing one of his Ohio State T-shirts he instantly understood the man's greeting. Then the guy said, "So how do ya' think we're gonna do this year?" and even though the football season was still over two months away Old Joe replied, "Oh, 'bout usual – I think we're gonna kick some ass."

Then the man chuckled and asked, "Are you goin' in?" as he put out his cigarette and held open the door. "Well, thank you kind sir," said Old Joe, and then the two men walked up as if they were no longer strangers and took a couple seats at the bar. There was an empty barstool standing in between the two of them so the man leaned across it to continue the conversation they'd begun outside.

"Wisconsin looks like they might be pretty good this year," he said, and Old Joe snapped back with "Aw, fuck Wisconsin," as he motioned down to "Billy W." to bring him a beer.

And when Billy arrived with his cold Coors Light Old Joe said, "Get this gentleman whatever he wants," to which the man responded, "Well thank you so much, it's been a long time since anyone has bought me a beer." Then he said, "By the way, my name is Hank," and as Old Joe reached out to shake his hand he replied, "I'm Joe, it's nice to meet ya."

"The pleasure's all mine," said Hank, and then he added, "You know, I always love meeting other Buckeye fans, because I could talk football every day of the year."

Then they began talking about the history of Ohio State football, about Vic Janowicz and "Hopalong" Cassady, about Eddie George and Archie Griffin, about Rex Kern and Chris Spielman. And they talked about Woody Hayes and Urban Meyer and about how they both hated "fucking Michigan," and about some of the Buckeye memorabilia they'd collected through the years and about some of the incredible games that they would never forget; the "10-10 tie" with "that team up north" in '73; the double-overtime win against Miami for the National Championship in '02; and the playoff wins just a few years back versus Alabama and Oregon while on their way to yet another national title.

And as the two men became more comfortable with one another they began to reveal those secret parts of their lives that only friends can discuss, like how Hank had been a Cleveland Browns fan for his entire life. To which Old Joe quipped, "Oh, shit pal, I'm sorry to hear that," because everyone on the planet knew that the Browns had been horrible for years. Then they talked about Brian

Sipe's "Red Right 88," and about "The Drive" and "The Fumble," and then Hank asked his new companion, "So what NFL team do you follow?" "Well," said Old Joe, "I can feel your pain because I've been a Lions fan my whole life." "The Lions," Hank exclaimed, "fucking Detroit?" "But they're in Michigan," he said, "and we hate fucking Michigan – so how can you like them?"

"Yeah, I know," replied Old Joe, "but the NFL is different, it's not like college where there's a state allegiance. Besides, my old man used to like them back in the day, back when they were great in the '50's." "Wait a minute," said Hank, "*who* was great in the '50's?"

"The *Browns* were great in the '50's."

And thus began the great debate about which one of these sad sack franchises – both having never played in a modern-day title game – had actually been better in the '50's, back when Old Joe was just a child and before Hank had even been born.

Hank said, "The Browns won three championships in the fifties, in '50, '54, and '55." And Old Joe retorted, "So did the Lions, in '52, '53, and '57." "Oh bullshit," said Hank. "Look it up," countered Old Joe, "It's true – as a matter of fact the Lions beat the Browns for every single one of their championships."

"Oh hell," said Hank, "I know you're right – I just don't like to think about it."

As it turns out, the Lions and Browns did indeed have quite a rivalry back in the 1950's. As both men stated, each team won three championships, with the Browns playing in seven championship games while the Lions played in four. And the Lions did in fact win all of their championships with the Browns as their opponent. In 1952, Detroit beat Cleveland by a score of 17-7, and then again the following year 17-16. But then Cleveland got their revenge that next year (in '54) by walloping the Lions 56-10. However, it still wasn't over, because a few years later (in 1957) Detroit got their revenge by pummeling the Browns 59-14.

Then as the two men began to now commiserate with one another about each of their team's lack of recent success, they continued pounding more beers until eventually coming back to the one thing that had originally brought them together – Ohio State football.

So they talked about the prospects for the upcoming season and which of their talented young men would start at quarterback, and then they talked about their running backs and their wide receivers and how they were going to reload on the defensive line and in the secondary.

(There's a saying at Ohio State: "We don't rebuild – we reload.")

And then they started talking about the Ohio State Marching Band (better known to Buckeye fans as "The Best Damn Band in the Land") and "Script Ohio" and the "skull session" and the exact history behind "Hang on Sloopy" before, Lord help us, they both began to sing:

Ha-aa-ang on Sloopy, bomp-bomp-bomp-bomp
ba ba bomp bomp bomp, ba ba bomp bomp bomp,
Ha-aa-ang on Sloopy, bomp-bomp-bomp-bomp
ba ba bomp bomp bomp, ba ba bomp bomp bomp ...

But they were just getting warmed up, because next came the Ohio State fight songs. First, was "Across the Field."

Fight the team across the field
Show them Ohio's here
Set the earth reverberating
With a mighty cheer
Rah! Rah! Rah!
Hit them hard and see how they fall,
Never let that team get the ball,
Hail, hail, the gang's all here,
So let's win that old conference now.

And then, of course, came the "Buckeye Battle Cry."

In old Ohio there's a team
That's known throughout the land,
Eleven warriors brave and bold
Whose fame will ever stand.
And when the ball goes over
Our cheers will reach the sky,
Ohio field will hear again
The Buckeye Battle Cry!
Drive, drive on down the field
Men of scarlet and gray,
Don't let them through that line
We've got to win this game today,
COME ON OHIO!
Smash through to victory
We cheer you as you go!
Our honor defend
We will fight to the end
For OHIO!

And there was no doubt about it. These two men were willing to "fight to the end" for their beloved Buckeyes.

But when they had finished singing and both had become even a little more drunk, Hank began to tell Old Joe the actual reason why he had come to Put-In-Bay that weekend. It seemed that Hank's only son was getting married that very next day and he had decided not to attend.

Old Joe couldn't believe what he was hearing.

"You're not going to the wedding?" he asked.

And then he added, "But he's your son."

"I know, I know," said Hank, "but you don't understand – the woman he's marrying is a bitch. I mean, she's a real fucking bitch Joe. My wife and I have tried again and again to be as nice as we can possibly be, and tried to be accommodating, you know, but it doesn't matter – nothing matters with her. She's just rude, and nasty, and mean – and the final straw came just a few days ago at the rehearsal dinner, because it turns out that her mother is even worse than she is! Anyway, to make a long story short, we were completely and utterly ignored – and my wife was in tears. And then, come to find out, they had changed where we were going to sit at the wedding reception. They were gonna move us to some back fucking table, if you can believe that, so that's when I said, 'Ok, enough is enough,' and decided not to attend."

"Wow," said Old Joe, "that's heart-breaking Hank – it truly is."

"Anyway," said Hank, "we were still moping around on Tuesday and Wednesday, so then yesterday I said to the wife, 'You know, fuck this, let's go to Put-In-Bay' – and so we did!" Then Hank let out a laugh. He had a great laugh, an unusual cackle, sort of like a mixture between a rooster and a hyena.

Then, as he continued to talk about his son, about how much he loved him and wanted him to be happy, Old Joe found himself thinking about Diago.

17.

It was somewhere around midnight and Old Joe was very drunk.

"I was talking about you today," he said. "Oh yeah," replied Diago, "only good stuff I hope." "Well, I was talking about you, or I was thinking about you probably, cause I was talkin' to this guy and we were talking about football and 'Do you like football?' oh, no, no, that's right, you don't like football you told me that – you like that other thing they call football but that's not football, that's some kind of 'pussy shit,' because football is about hitting people and blocking and tackling and … you should like football Diago you really should because it's American, and I want you to like that ok? I think you should because, that's a good thing, and you should get married and have a whole shitload of kids that drive you fucking insane because that's what it's all about you know – Where's your girlfriend? You have a girlfriend don't you – you don't? I thought you did, yeah, you had a girlfriend – sure ya' did – what? You broke up? Well, what's your fucking problem then, there's a whole island full of beautiful women just go pick one out for Christ's sake – Diago, are you listening? Don't end up like me Diago, don't end up like me because

49

you're young and then you're old and time flies – do you know what I mean? No, you don't know what I mean but you will – you will, and that's what I mean – don't fuck around, do you hear?"

Then Old Joe put his head down on the bar and began mumbling, "You're a good kid Diago, you're a real good kid, don't end up like me – you're better than that."

Diago went around to the other side of the bar to try to help his friend get to his feet, "Come on Old Joe, I think you've had enough for one night. Would you like me to call you a cab?"

"What? I'm ok, I'm ok, I'm – just let me sit here a minute."

Then Old Joe got to his feet and began walking out of Mojito Bay.

The sand was making it more difficult for him to keep his balance, but he made it out of the bar. Then, he turned right and proceeded southward on Catawba.

Eventually, he would make it all the way back to his motel room.

18.

"Well, well, well," said Old Joe, "look who's here."

It was Walter the dog, back again, and bouncing his way into Frosty's.

He trotted down the length of the bar and went right on up to Old Joe, so that the old man could give him a scratch behind the ear, and then he went down the hallway toward the back patio and was gone – just as suddenly as he had appeared.

And for that brief, shining moment, Walter had made Old Joe's day. Because, to be honest, he sometimes liked dogs more than he did people, though he'd never been too crazy about cats. There was one exception to this rule however – as is usually the case – and it came in the form of a little kitten with "whom" he'd had a chance encounter years before.

Old Joe was young back then (somewhere in his late teens or maybe even his early twenties) and was working on one of the odd jobs that he would often take in order to pay his way through college. There'd been quite a few of them over the years, including some roofing and painting jobs along with some construction work. But he spent one summer delivering flowers.

And one morning, while he was loading his van, he heard a strange sound.

He couldn't figure out what it was or where it was coming from, so he continued on with his work. Then once the van had been loaded and he was "set-up" for his deliveries – with his cardboard map well-routed with colored pins and with the scrap paper on his clipboard duly numbered – he went to start the engine. But, in one of the rare instances, it didn't turn over on the first attempt, and that's when Old Joe heard that strange noise again – though he still didn't have a clue as to what it was or where it was coming from.

So he hopped out of the van and began to investigate. And lo and behold, wedged between the concrete of the alleyway and his driver's side front tire was an emaciated kitten, and he was making little sounds that were more like chirps than meows – and if that van had moved even an inch it would have most assuredly crushed him to death.

And when Old Joe went to pick him up he said, "Boy, you sure are lucky," so that became his name, "Lucky." But at that moment, he sure didn't look like it. He stayed motionless in Old Joe's hands and was barely breathing. So he carried Lucky back to the loading dock and found a cardboard box in which to lay him down. He lined it with newspaper to make him more comfortable and filled a little plastic cup with water (which was actually the top piece of a floral container) to see if he would drink. But Lucky wouldn't, or perhaps couldn't; he just lied there close to death. He was a handsome kitten with brownish-orange fur and he had white mittens for paws, though if he didn't eat soon he was going to perish.

Old Joe knew that if his boss saw Lucky he wouldn't like it very much, so he put the cardboard box in a spare room in the back where most of the employees rarely went and then left to find some food. He was already running late on his route for the day but he knew that Lucky required some nourishment immediately.

So he jumped in his van (which started right up) and he went flying down the back alley. He knew a shortcut to a nearby carry-out and he was there in no time flat. He ran into the store and went up and down the aisles frantically searching for some kind of pet food and though he couldn't find any "cat food" he did see a can of tuna fish and thought, *"Ok, that'll work."* So he purchased the tuna fish along with a can opener and then ran back and jumped into his van and in less than two minutes he was slamming his brakes at the flower shop.

Then he hurried back into the room where he'd left the little kitten to see if he was still alive, but Lucky wasn't moving and it was hard to tell if he was breathing. So he opened up the can of tuna fish and put it into the cardboard box next to Lucky. Then, after a few seconds, the little guy began to slowly move his head – he'd caught a whiff. And then, incredibly, that tiny lifeless ball of fur suddenly sprang to his feet and devoured the entire can of tuna in about three seconds flat!

Old Joe couldn't believe it. That little kitten had instantly come to life and for the first he saw what a truly gorgeous creature he really was – and what a personality! He was *so* expressive, with his big green eyes now looking up at Old Joe and asking for more food. "You want some more fella?" asked Old Joe, "Ok, you wait here and I'll be right back." And Lucky sat right back down in his cardboard box like a perfect little gentleman.

Now, at that point, if he'd been thinking straight he would've simply taken the kitten with him for a ride in the van. But, he was just so damned happy that Lucky was alive, he went by himself instead – and once more flew down that alleyway and back in record time.

And when he came back, he had *two* cans of tuna fish.

He was hoping that Lucky would still be there and that he hadn't wandered off – and thankfully, when he went into the backroom and looked inside that cardboard box, there he was, his new little buddy, sitting and patiently waiting. Then Old Joe opened another can and put it down next to Lucky, and once again he devoured it, though not quite as quickly as he had before.

Old Joe took this to be a good sign.

It looked like Lucky was back to full speed. Only, now what? Old Joe wasn't sure what his next move should be, whether he should leave Lucky in the backroom all day or take him along as he made his deliveries. But he knew that he'd better do something soon or he'd be out of a job.

He was running terribly late.

Though, as is sometimes the case, his decision was made for him. Because right at that moment, as he was standing there and pondering his next move, another employee of the flower shop opened the door to the backroom and startled Lucky. In an instant, that little kitten leaped onto Old Joe's pant leg and scurried up his back to lay himself behind his neck. So there he was – his back legs were on Old Joe's left shoulder and his front legs were on his right and the kitten's head was tucked right up underneath the young man's face – as they both looked to see who the person was that had entered the room.

Fortunately, for both of them, it was Laurie; a nice young woman who worked as a floral designer at the shop. "Oh my goodness," she said, "who in the world do you have there?" "This is Lucky," answered Old Joe as he went on to tell her what had all taken place. "Well if that isn't just the most adorable thing that I have ever seen in my whole life," she said, "the way he cuddles around your neck like that – but hey, you'd better get outta here, you're late." Then she added, "Don't worry, I won't say anything."

So away they went – Old Joe and Lucky.

And for the next several hours, the young flower delivery man had a new partner as they drove all around northwestern Ohio – and whenever Old Joe would go to leave the van, Lucky would crawl back into that same position behind his neck to come along.

And even Old Joe had to admit, it was just the cutest damned thing.

The two of them had formed an instant bond. They were best friends.

You could even say that Old Joe, who had never much cared for cats before this, actually loved that little kitten. And how could he not? Because, as he saw it, any animal that would show this much trust in someone simply had to be loved.

However, there was a problem. At the time, Old Joe lived in a duplex that didn't allow pets, and this was on his mind as they were finishing their deliveries for the day. He would look over at that tiny creature sitting in the passenger's seat and say, "So Lucky, what are we gonna do now buddy? What are we gonna do?" But, once again, it was Laurie to the rescue. As it turned out, she lived on a farm with plenty of open space and she said that she'd be more than happy to take Lucky home with her.

Thus, the two new friends had to say good-bye.

But, every now and then, Old Joe would ask about his old partner and Laurie would always report that he was doing "just fine" – that he was happy and healthy and getting along well with all of the other animals – and that would put a smile on the young delivery man's face.

And for the rest of his life, even though Old Joe would always remain partial to dogs, he would remember the day when he'd been able to rescue that very special little kitten.

The one he so aptly named.

19.

It was only eleven o'clock in the morning but Old Joe already had a nice little buzz going. That's because instead of having just one of "Eddie B's" fabulous Bloody Marys, or perhaps stopping at two, he was well into his third. And as he was sitting there at the Beer Barrel on one of his favorite barstools in the whole wide world and feeling that cool breeze wash over him again and again, a twin-engine prop went flying over the island and a thought crossed his mind that had occurred to him many times before:

"I am no different than any other human being who has ever walked upon the face of this earth and dreamt of flying ..."

And yet, he had never flown.

(That's if you didn't include that one time when he was five and went soaring over his house in a small plane with his parents and baby brother – because Old Joe didn't have a memory of ever having done it.)

This thought was obviously the result of having been a history teacher for many years – and having at least a working knowledge of how we as human beings had gotten to this collective point. So, after taking another sip of his half-finished Bloody Mary, he leaned back in his barstool and pretended that he was lecturing in class again. He continued:

... this includes, of course, all of those who tilted their heads back and stared into space prior to the Wright Brothers taking flight at Kitty Hawk, those people who lived during the nineteenth and eighteenth centuries and every proceeding century for two million years, all the way back to the cavemen of the Paleolithic Age, although, they didn't actually live in caves – a misnomer, one which has often been mis-understood – for they were hunters and gatherers who had to search for their food and, therefore, were simply not afforded the luxury of a permanent settlement.

Like Monticello, for instance, the magnificent home of another non-flyer by the name of Thomas Jefferson – a renaissance man if ever there was one – though, not of the Renaissance Age itself, exactly, but rather a distinguished gentleman of the so-called Enlightenment Period; ah yes, the illustrious Mr. Jefferson, who became not only the celebrated author of the world famous Declaration of Independence, and the third President of the United States, but also a scientist, an architect, an inventor, and a food and wine connoisseur, among his many other note-worthy accomplishments.

But even this man, with all of his fame, was really no different than you and I, for we are all human beings, and we have all walked on this same planet, thus, we have all had a dream to fly – though some of us never do. And that's the beautiful thing about history because ... um, wait a minute. You know, now that I think of it, I remember reading somewhere that Jefferson once took a ride in a hot-air balloon while he was living in Paris. So, in a sense, I guess he did fly.

Furthermore, I think that it's also safe to assume that at least one homo erectus, perhaps while chasing a prehistoric gazelle or wooly mammoth, fell off a cliff and went "flying" to his death; however, not like in the movies, where some "caveman" is always being carried off in the beak of a Pterodactyl – with dinosaurs by that time having already been extinct for approximately 65 million years – but here's the thing ..."

That's when he heard that hollow sound coming through the straw. His glass was empty. So he flagged down "Eddie B." and ordered his fourth giant-sized Bloody Mary of the morning.

Then he tried to remember where he'd left off.

Oh boy, he was really flying now.

20.

For some people, living in a bar town like Put-In-Bay might've tended to get rather monotonous, but for a drunk like Old Joe it was a natural fit and suited him right down to the ground. Most of the denizens who actually stayed on the island were either employees or locals with money, and those wealthier ones usually resided along the western parts and weren't generally inclined to frequent the downtown bars.

So the town in the summer was inhabited mostly by tourists who would usually leave on the same day they arrived, and at times it was as if the previous day had never happened because there would be no one left to remember. And the days had a way of blending into one another like waves washing over the beach, thus Old Joe just wanted to stay there forever so that his sins, like footprints, could fade away.

But even though for the most part he was an ornery old cuss who drank and swore and gambled, by now most of the workers were familiar with his story and felt like he was a person that they could trust. They knew he'd been born in Ohio and had lived here his whole life and was raised in a middle-class family, and that he'd worked several jobs to put himself through college and then had taught for many years in a public school. And he was a Buckeyes fan, just like they were, and though at times he could be somewhat obnoxious, Old Joe was a native son who'd been accepted as one of their own and he had become a constant presence on South Bass Island.

21.

On a somewhat balmy June afternoon while having a beer over at Frosty's, Old Joe was watching this timid young man trying his damnedest to meet a pretty girl. He had inched his way across the floor after being coaxed along relentlessly by his buddies, then as the drama unfolded and he'd finally reached his target he was going in for the attempted landing.

So he tapped her on the shoulder and they shared some small talk and for a moment she actually appeared to smile, but then for some strange reason when extending his hand he said, "Hi, my name is David Allen Smith."

"Oh for Christ's sake kid," thought Old Joe, *"you've got to be fucking kidding me."*

Now the old man considered himself to be an expert on names, being both a history teacher and of Polish descent, so as he watched the poor kid begin to crash and then burn he thought, *"Why in the world did you have to say Allen?"*

And with a last name like "Smith" he did have some sympathy for the kid, since he may've just been trying to set himself apart, but mostly he considered the use of a middle name to be nothing more than ostentatious. Old Joe thought it was better when people would try to hide their middle names like they used to do back in grade school, though at the same time he absolutely loved all of those "classics" that he had learned about down through history. Like Henry Wadsworth Longfellow and Samuel Langhorne Clemens and Oliver Hazard Perry and William Tecumseh Sherman, but as he sat there waiting for "Johnny B. Goode" to serve him another beer he began to think, *"Though what about all of those assassins?"*

Such as John Wilkes Booth and Lee Harvey Oswald and Mark David Chapman and James Earl Ray, then he wondered if any of them had ever used *their* middle names when trying to pick up a pretty girl.

Then he thought about some of those serial killers he'd heard of like John Wayne Gacy and Paul John Knowles and God only knows about how many others, then he glanced back around at "Mr. David Allen Smith" and gave him a more thorough "once over."

And for the briefest of moments he thought about going up to young David and trying to help the kid work it all out, but he didn't want to come off as some kind of "know-it-all" once again, so he just leaned back in his barstool and drank his beer.

22.

It was late in the evening but Diago had the night off so Old Joe had already left Mojito Bay, and since he wasn't sure exactly where to go he headed north before ending up at The Boardwalk.

He had a few beers on "the upper deck" as it was called by a railing that overlooked the water, but then he had a taste for one of those reddish-orange drinks with those names he had such trouble remembering.

There was a nice young woman working behind the bar and she made him a smallish Hurricane, then he went walking past the fancy shop windows and began perusing some of the items. So he was just sauntering along sipping on his drink (that had been conveniently transferred into a plastic cup) when he looked inside a closed ice cream parlor window and noticed an "OPEN" sign that was used during business.

And though the lights were turned off it reminded him of another one that he used to see on his way to work, and he recalled how he would always be sure to glance over as he drove by that same building each morning.

Then in his last years of teaching how those beguiling red letters began to entice him more and more, as they went rhythmically blinking before flashing in unison inside the window of that Local 14.

"O – P – E – N."

"OPEN."

How he would take that right onto Northover across from the factory then drive by around 7:15, and only wish he had the time to sit down next to a "third-shifter" for some good conversation and a morning beer. But then, as always, to make himself feel better he would think, *"Maybe someday – when I retire,"* as he now passed a receptacle and tossed in his empty cup and then continued along on his way.

And as he walked toward Catawba to go southward up the hill and then however slowly back to his motel room, he couldn't help but think of all of the bullshit he'd endured to finally end up here at Put-In-Bay.

A smile crept upon the old man's face.

23.

It was almost ten when Old Joe arrived at the Beer Barrel, having walked through the shadiness of its inner sanctum, past the vending machines that aligned the hallway, and then out into that majestic openness toward the longest bar in the entire world.

"Eddie B." saw him coming and began his usual preparations of a Bloody Mary, a Coors Light, a Diet Coke, and a water and said, "Hey Joe, so how we doin' this mornin'?"

He grabbed a Coors Light out of the cooler with one hand and quickly poured a glass of water with the other, while Old Joe sat down on his favorite barstool and said, "Oh, pretty good, considering the way I feel – how 'bout yourself?"

"Oh, not bad," replied Eddie, "can't complain." Then he saw Old Joe put a book on the bar and asked, "What's that you got there?"

"It's a book," said the old man.

"Yeah, I can see that – but what kind of book?"

"Aw hell, I don't know."

"You don't know? What do you mean you don't know? It's your book – isn't it?"

Then Old Joe picked up the book and looked at the cover and said, "Not really, a waitress gave it to me last night – says the main character reminds her an awful lot of me – and I guess she wants me to read it and then discuss it with her or somethin'. Who knows?"

"Oh yeah?" said Eddie, "Well it sounds like this waitress is a little sweet on ya' buddy, you better watch yourself – what's her name?"

"Nah, it's nothing like that – her name's Sarita. She works over at The Boathouse."

"No kidding? So what's the title of the book?"

Then Old Joe looked at the cover again and said, "It's called, 'On the Other Side of Poughkeepsie.'"

And then Eddie started laughing and said, "Oh, good luck with that one," to which Old Joe rather sarcastically replied, "Yeah, well, how bad can it be?" "I don't know," said Eddie, "but I know this much – if she wants you to read it, then she probably wants to talk to you about it tonight – so you'd better get crackin'." Then Eddie started laughing again as he walked away and Old Joe said to himself, "Shit – he's right."

"She's probably gonna expect me to have this whole damned thing read by tonight, because that's how women are – if they want somethin' done, they want it done now," he thought.

Then Old Joe started to panic a little bit, *"Just what in the world have I gotten myself into anyway? Maybe I can get someone to read it for me, maybe 'Eddie B.' – no, wait, he's too busy."* Then he continued, *"I just wanna drink. Why can't people leave me be?"* But, after pausing for a moment, he thought, *"Ok, look, she's a really sweet girl. So why don't you just read the damn book?"*

Then he softly repeated to himself, "After all, how bad can it be?"

So, with his four drinks in front of him, Old Joe opened the book and began to read:

It was early morning and once again Nicholas couldn't sleep. He felt trapped. His bedroom, once a sanctuary, had become his prison. He had to get out, a feeling that was not uncommon.

"Oh Christ," thought Old Joe, *"I hate this already."* But, thinking of Sarita, he continued.

He'd escaped this bedroom, and its female sentries, many times before. However, these were facts of which Nicholas was no longer proud, and in his mind these incidents had been far removed, ever since his marriage to Jennifer. Never before had a woman been so at ease with his manner and she was the only woman with whom he had shared the word "love." Though, his infamous exits, now graceful and refined, had for some reason begun to happen once more. He waited for Jennifer's breathing to suggest departure, then slowly raised her arm from his waist, carefully slid from underneath the flannel sheets, and quietly left the room.

"Holy shit," thought Old Joe, *"what drivel."*

So he decided to skip ahead a few pages.

He was out of shape, so the short run had made him breathe heavy. "Through the nose and out the mouth," he thought. After all, that's the correct way, the air's more refreshing, more relaxing. He wondered how many people in the world practiced this technique, then he wondered how many people were breathing through the nose and out the mouth at that very moment. Then he wondered how many of those people were thinking like he was at that moment, thinking if other people were breathing through the nose and out the mouth like they were. But then, by thinking this, he thought himself to be strange.

He sometimes thought himself to be a genius, entertaining thoughts no one else in the world had ever had and thinking about things that might be considered unusual, while contemplating ideas unfamiliar to mankind. At other times, sometimes the very next moment, he'd consider himself the dumbest person to have ever lived. However, there were these other times when he simply thought himself to be strange. This was one of those times.

Old Joe paused and said to himself, "That's because you *are* strange – you asshole."

Then he skipped ahead a whole lot of pages.

He walked farther down the street and then into an alley, which is what he preferred, passing the backsides of the Quick-Six mini-mart, The First National Bank, and Ollies Tavern, then through the parking lot of the adult theatre and past the post office, then under a tortured piece of sheet metal which failed to block his access to a narrow passageway between The Country Peddler Flower Shop and the Coin-O-Matic laundromat, where he glanced inside the window to see a lonely old man folding clothes. He then crossed two additional sidestreets with intermittent jogging before once more finding the shelter of trees, driveways, porchlights, and crabgrass, and all the rest that to him constituted a real neighborhood.

Old Joe put a napkin on the page as a marker and then closed the book.

"Ok," he said, "this is brutal."

Then he raised his voice a little louder to make sure that Eddie would hear him and said, "This is awful!"

Then "Eddie B." walked by with a smile and said, "So, how are things goin'?" "Oh brother," answered the old man, "this is freaking torture." Eddie started to laugh again. "I'm not kiddin'," said Old Joe, "I mean – it's really bad! It's about some guy walking around thinking about bullshit."

"Oh yeah," said Eddie, trying not to laugh, "and what else?"

"No, that's it – that's all there is – it's horrible."

And at that point, Eddie was almost in hysterics, "Be sure to let me know how that goes for ya'," he said, now pretending to double over as he walked away.

Then Old Joe sat there for a moment and had a sip of his Diet Coke, then he took a nice long drink from his Bloody Mary, and then he took an even longer drink from his Coors Light, followed by a sip from his glass of water.

And then he looked down at the book and thought, "*Oh, what the hell, if Sarita wants me to read this shit then, ok – that's fine.*" Then he opened to the bookmark, skipped a few more pages ahead, let out a sigh, and continued:

Nicholas was a complicated mixture of cockiness and self-doubt. He pictured himself walking on a never-ending high wire, precariously balanced between insensitivity on one side and insecurity on the other, with that two-headed monster anxiously prowling the cavernous pit below and prepared to swallow him whole should he fall on either side. And even if he didn't fall, even if he was on his best behavior and did everything right, it was as if his blanket of self-assuredness was never quite long enough to totally mask one creature without at least partially exposing the other, and he simply couldn't put the monster to sleep. For Nicholas, it was a constant struggle.

"Oh my goodness," thought Old Joe, "get to the verb!"

So, once again, he skipped a few pages.

After all, that's what mattered most to Nicholas, not so much the winning, but rather the attempt. And it's not that he was a good sport, because he certainly wasn't a good loser, not at all. Instead, he was a familiar one, for he had lost more than he had won, and perhaps this is the reason why it was easier for him to accept. However, until that one evening, he had never walked away from a fight.

And then, he skipped a few more.

Once, feeling awkward, but also feeling compelled to do so, Nicholas looked up the word "love" in a dictionary; it read, "to freely accept another in loyalty." He had always remembered this definition but believed it to be a contradiction – and was now feeling more obliged than ever to both question and disagree. "If you 'freely' accept someone, then why must they be loyal? That is, if you accept someone warts and all, why must they be faithful? On the other hand, if someone is unfaithful, does this disprove their love, and should it diminish yours for them? And what if a person is faithful, what does that prove?" Because even though Nicholas had always been faithful to Jennifer, he wondered, "Does this prove my love? There's got to be more to it," he thought. "Do people who write dictionaries really know about love? And if so, are they the only ones?"

"Or could it be that no one knows?"

And then Old Joe skipped ahead to almost the very end of the book and thought, *"Ok, for my darling Sarita, I'll give it one last try."* Then he took a big gulp of his Bloody Mary, finished his Coors Light, and continued.

"The truth is I love her. The truth is I can't understand why she loves me. The truth is she's the best thing that's ever happened to me. The truth is I have never felt worthy of her love." He crouched down beside the railroad tracks, then put one knee on the ground. He took long, deep breaths, before finally standing up straight with hands on hips. He could now see his breath in the air and remembered how it always seemed to be cooler here by the lumber yard. *"She's known all along,"* thought Nicholas, *"that I love her, just as I know that she loves me. Otherwise, she would have never put up with my foolish antics. So when she smiled and kissed me on the cheek that night, she wasn't trying to belittle me, or embarrass me. She wouldn't do that.*

She did it, quite simply, because she loves me.

Because she wanted to protect me. Just as I wanted to protect her.

She was probably saying, 'Hey, I know that you're an idiot, but I love you anyway, and even though you deserve a good ass-kicking, I'm going to save you because you're my husband.'

And let's face it, I would've gotten my ass kicked – that guy was huge!

But that's why I didn't understand her actions, because I've never really understood love; though Jennifer has known what it is all along. Love isn't about saying, or thinking, or even giving or receiving. Because, when it's all said and done, love is simply love."

Nicholas stood there.

He was now feeling guilty for having questioned Jennifer's love.

"How in the world has she ever put up with me," he thought.

Then suddenly, he realized himself to once again be the luckiest man on the face of the earth – a thought which he truly believed to not be an exaggeration – and decided from that point on to simply count his immense blessings and be grateful. So, after vowing to never again take Jennifer for granted, he turned around, took a refreshingly deep breath, and with a smile on his face began the long journey back home.

Old Joe closed the book and tossed it onto the bar.

"Ok," he said, "that is without a doubt the biggest piece of horseshit that I have ever read." At this point, a few other people were sitting at the bar and Eddie said, "Oh, come on Joe, tell us how you *really* feel." Then, in a voice that was a bit more subdued, the old man leaned onto the bar a little ways and said, "Eddie, if anything, I'm being too kind – seriously."

Then Eddie said, "Well, at least you read it. That's the important thing"

"Yeah, or parts of it anyways," said Old Joe with a little chuckle, "but it's like you said – tonight, when she asks me, I'll have something to say."

"That's right," said Eddie, "don't worry my friend, you'll do fine."

"Well, we'll see buddy – we'll see."

And as Old Joe sat there he thought, *"At least I know the names of the main characters – Nicholas and Jennifer."*

Then he kept on thinking,

"Nicholas and Jennifer."

"Nicholas and Jennifer."

"Just remember, Nicholas and Jennifer."

24.

Later that day, after he'd visited his other designated establishments, and on yet another magical Put-In-Bay evening, Old Joe went to The Boathouse.

As he walked in, though he didn't see Sarita right off, he spotted something else that was rather enticing – an honest to goodness barstool. One had just opened up in the place where he hadn't been able to get a seat at the bar for weeks. So, as quickly as he could (which really wasn't all that fast anymore), the old man bounced off a few would-be defenders and went breaking through the line and after finding some open field – just like in his playing days at St. Ignatius – he scored a touchdown.

Then, after taking a moment to properly adjust himself on one of those "thrones" that he had coveted for so long, he flagged down the barkeep for a bottle of Coors Light and started looking around to find Sarita. Like waitresses at most bars and restaurants, Sarita had her own section; although, at The Boathouse, things were a little more casual and she could usually roam about. So Old Joe was into his second beer before he saw her and when she spotted him she smiled and waved and then held up a finger as to suggest, *Just a second – I'll be right there.* And when she got the chance she walked over to see him and said, "Wow Papa, a seat at the bar, that's pretty impressive – I have to say," and he responded with, "Well, there she is, 'The Waitress of the Year,' or should I say my 'Temptress of the Night.'"

"Oh, you stop that now," she said.

Somewhere along the way, they had started to refer to each other by different nicknames, though it was pretty obvious that she didn't much care for his whole "Temptress of the Night" thing, so Old Joe immediately made a "note to self" – *never use that nickname again.* On the other hand, though he always loved hearing the sound of her sultry voice, this was especially so when she was saying his name – and he secretly adored whenever she called him "Papa" (which had jokingly begun a few weeks earlier because of the ever-present "Papa Lou's" cap he liked to wear.)

"So," she continued, "did you get a chance to start reading that book?"

"Well," said Old Joe, sounding quite proud of himself, "funny you should ask – because yes, I did."

"Oh really, how exciting – so how far did you get?"

"Uh, well, I finished it."

"You finished it? In one day?"

"Well, yeah," said Old Joe, "pretty much I did."

"Pretty much? Come on Papa, how much is pretty much?"

"Well …"

"Are you lying? Did you even read it at all?"

"Yes, yes, I read it, of course I did – it's about Nicholas and Jennifer, right?"

"Really?" said Sarita, "ok, then what did you think of it?"

"Um, well, it was really somethin'."

"Oh Papa, why are you doing this?"

"Doing what?"

Then Sarita put her hand on his shoulder and said, "Look, if you don't like it, you don't have to read it."

And Old Joe said, "It's not that, it's just …"

"Papa, I won't be disappointed, ok? If you don't want to read it, that's fine. But if you do want to read it, just take your time and relax – there's no pressure." And as she began to walk away she looked back at him and said, "Hakuna matata." Then, with her usual grace, she gave him a little smile, turned, and went on her way.

And as Old Joe watched her disappear back into the crowd he said to himself, "Wow, what a woman."

25.

It was about one o'clock in the morning and Old Joe was talking to his friend Diago at Mojito Bay. He was telling the young bartender about what happened earlier that evening with Sarita – how she had left him sitting there speechless with his mouth agape – while having a few more beers before closing time.

Diago listened intently.

Then he asked, "So what does she look like?"

"Well," said a somewhat reticent Old Joe, for not wanting to be too descriptive, "she's darker than chocolate and sweeter than candy – she's tall and slender with a terrific smile – and there's nary a mean bone in that gorgeous body of hers." And then he told Diago that she was one of the nicest people he'd ever met but he never had a clue as to what she was going to say next.

"Ok, wait a minute," said Diago, "so you're telling me that, as she was walking away, she looked back at you and actually said the words, 'Hakuna matata?'"

"Yep, that's what she said all right."

"Wow, that's pretty cool."

"Yeah, I know."

Fortunately, the bar was less crowded than usual, as Old Joe continued on about Sarita, explaining once more about how she'd given him that book to read the evening before.

"Man Old Joe," said Diago, "you're in some trouble here."

"Whaddaya mean?"

"Are you kidding? She wants you man."

"Oh bullshit."

But Diago insisted, "No, I'm telling you – she does."

"Oh, gimme a break, will ya' Diago – I'm old enough to be her grandfather for Christ's sake."

"That doesn't matter," said Diago, "look, I'm sorry to be the one to have to tell you this, but age has got nothin' to do with it – no one gets to choose when they fall in love."

"Love? Who in the hell said anything about love? Like I've been tellin' people, it's nothing like that – we're just good friends."

"Yeah, right, and since you sat down here all you've been talking about is this girl – Sarita this and Sarita that – so who you kiddin'?"

"Diago, listen to what I'm saying – there's nothin' to it, ok?"

"Ok buddy, have it your way – but you're missin' the boat here, I'm tellin' ya."

"Duly noted," said Old Joe.

Then Diago started to laugh and said, "Man Old Joe, you sure do get around – you must know everyone in town."

"Me?" said the old man with a chuckle. "No kid, hardly."

"Sure you do – you know what? You should run for mayor."

"Oh brother," said Old Joe.

"Why not? I think it's a great idea."

"Yeah, that's the problem, you and your great ideas. Look kid, I don't think you've thought this one through very well – after all, just how many years do you think I've got left?"

"Oh, that's ok," said Diago, as he began to laugh again, "cuz when you die we can just prop you up with a cane in the corner over there – or better yet, you can be like a ghost and go floating around and watch over everyone on the island – I'll tell ya' what, alive or dead, you got my vote."

Then Old Joe said, "So that's it huh? A ghost mayor? That's your great idea?"

"Well," said Diago, "at least you have a goal now – right?"

"Boy, you're just 'Mr. Funny Man' tonight aren't ya'?"

"Book in advance," shouted Diago as he began to walk away, "I'll be here all week."

"Good my friend," said Old Joe, then after taking a swig of his beer he quietly added, "because that's what I'm countin' on."

26.

Last night, Old Joe had a dream.

He was about nine years old and was sitting with his dad at Tiger Stadium watching the Lions play the Bears.

The gigantic scoreboard above the bleachers was showing all of the other scores from all of the other games in all of the other cities, and he was there in Detroit – sitting next to his dad.

And the stadium had those wonderful smells like it used to have, of all that cheap-ass cigar smoke and so many spilt beers, and he felt more love than he had ever known before – because, more than anything, he felt protected.

By his father, by the stadium, and perhaps by the Almighty himself.

For it seemed as if God had taken that entire city into the palms of his hands, given it as good shake, and made it snow – just for them.

And this had made the little boy happy.

He had never been so happy.

But suddenly, everyone vanished, and the little boy was left sitting there all alone. Then the next thing he knew, he was an old man again, standing outside and looking in at the stadium – which now laid in ruins.

There was a partial shell with some pillars and posts that had somehow moved to Toledo and stood next to his childhood home. And as he encircled the catacombs of the tunnels and the sarcophagus of the right field stands, at first he couldn't find a way in, and then he couldn't find a way out – and all he really knew for sure was that the little boy was lost.

After he'd awakened, he sat up in bed for a few minutes thinking about the dream. Then he finished what was left of his warm beer that had been sitting on the nightstand, laid himself back down, and went to sleep.

27.

Old Joe was back at Frosty's on a sunny afternoon with a gentle breeze blowing in off the back patio, and he'd just ordered another round of drinks for his new friends Bud and Marie, a retired mechanic and housewife from Middleburg Heights, about twenty miles southwest of Cleveland.

"We've been together for 45 years," said Marie, and Bud added, "yeah, and about 30 of those have been pretty good too," then Marie nudged her elbow into his side and said, "now you hush up," and both of them chuckled. "How about you Joe," asked Marie, "are you married?"

"Nope," said Old Joe, "never been."

"So you were too fast for any of 'em to catch ya' huh?" asked Bud. "Nah," said Old Joe, "I just never wanted that ol' ball and chain around my ankle I guess." Then he turned to Marie and said, "Sorry, just kidding." And Marie said, "Oh, that's all right hon, I hear it all the time from Bud's friends."

Then they all started sharing their stories about when they had come to "The Bay" for the first time. Marie remembered their family picnic and how delicious the chicken had been, and even though that had taken place back in the eighties she said that every time since she's made it a special point to have lunch at the Chicken Patio.

And then she asked each of the fellas if they happened to remember the first bar that they went to on the island, and Bud said, "Hmm, I was here about a year or two before we met dear so that was a while ago, what, about '72? But I think it had to be The Boathouse because I remember getting off the bus and walking down Toledo Avenue there, though what I recall more than anything was the weather and the people – and just how nice the day was – kinda like today."

"Aw, aren't you a sweetheart," said Marie, "you see why I love him Joe? So, what about you, what was the first bar that you remember walking into?"

"That's easy," he replied, "it was this one right here – Frosty's, without a doubt." Then she asked, "How can you be so certain?" And Old Joe said, "Oh, I could never forget that day, it's tattooed on my brain – but I don't think it was quite as innocent as Bud's first trip here." "Oh yeah, how so?" asked Bud. "Well, it was raining, and I mean it was coming down like cats and dogs when we got off the bus and I remember that we were just looking for shelter because, the thing is, we didn't know where in the hell we were going since none of us had ever been here before, and we were just runnin' around like a bunch of chickens with their heads cut off when we happened upon this place and came in to take cover. But what I remember most, and will never forget, were the 'beer slides.'"

Then he pointed and said, "Right over there."

"Beer slides?" asked Marie. "What in the world are those?"

Old Joe smiled and said, "All right, let me see if I can explain this – so my buddies and I were standing in that corner over there and, like I said, we had just gotten off the bus after taking the ferry ride over here and we were wet and tired and quite frankly I was bored, because, this place was dead. I mean, there was nothin' goin' on.

So then I turned to Bob, who was one of my buddies at the time and said, 'This is it? This is the great Put-In-Bay that I've heard so much about?' Because it was eleven in the morning and it was pouring outside and we were in a half-empty bar called 'Frosty's.' And to be honest, I was thinking about what time would be best to hop on the ferry and head back home. But, as luck would have it, a few minutes later some girls came in from out of the rain and when they took off their slickers, well, all of the young fellas in this place had heart attacks, including me, because these were three of the finest looking young women that you'd ever want to see. They were from somewhere in Indiana, as I recall, and they were wearing those cut-off shorts and tank tops that they wore back then and were kinda showin' off a lot of what God gave em', if you know what I mean. Anyway, as you might imagine, all the guys in the bar were trying their best to get to know these young ladies just a little bit better, but no one was having much luck.

Then an older fella stood up, though, heck, lookin' back, he couldn't of been much more than thirty-five or so, but he seemed pretty old to me at the time because – and Bud you'll like this – he was wearing one of those blue denim shirts, you know, the kind that mechanics wear with their name stitched onto the pocket. Well, he got up from his barstool and he had a cigarette in his mouth I remember because he was somehow able to keep it in there while he was talkin', ya' know, he was one of those guys – now this is back when it was still ok to smoke in public, right?

Anyway, he had a pitcher of beer in his hand and he said, 'Hey girls, have any of you ever done a 'Put-In-Bay beer slide?"

So then Bud, Marie, I shit you not, in one motion he swung his arm back and let that beer go – and it went flooding all across the floor up there by the bar, where those guys are, right over there, and then he turned to the girls and said, 'Well, there you go little ladies – unless you're chicken.' And then some other guy stood up and said, 'Wait a minute, if we're gonna do this thing, let's do it right,' then he poured his pitcher of beer on the floor as well, and I'm tellin' ya', in an instant, this place was electric and all eyes turned to those three young women. And two of them, right away, you could tell just by their hand gestures were like, *'No way, we don't want any part of this,'* but their blonde friend looked at the guys who were sitting at the bar and said, 'What? You want me to slide on that?' And the mechanic guy said, 'Yep, just like you're goin' into second base.' Then she shrugged her shoulders and said, 'Oh, what the hell.' And then she took a few steps back by this pool table over here and took off runnin' – and I mean to tell you that she slid on her ass all the way to the door.

And this place went nuts.

And from that moment on, I had an absolute blast – and I've been havin' one ever since. I remember saying to myself, 'Now this is the Put-In-Bay that I've heard so much about!' So then, of course, her friends had to do it as well and by that time the cow had left the barn because everybody and their sisters were running up and sliding and spilling more beer, including yours truly."

"That, my friend, is one helluva story," said Bud.

"All true," said Old Joe, "except, the funny thing is, after that first incredible slide, when that pretty blonde went whooshing all the way to the door, everyone else who tried it mostly just tumbled – and once again, I'm speaking from personal experience. But ever since the moment when that cute little ass of hers touched down and went sliding across this very floor, I've been in love with Frosty's Bar and Put-In-Bay."

"And you know what else I remember?"

"What's that?" asked Marie.

"The sun came out – and it turned into a beautiful day."

28.

Old Joe's eyesight was failing. Somedays were better than others, but over the past year it had gotten progressively worse. He didn't own a pair of prescription glasses for the simple reason that he had never needed them before, or had the occasion to wear them, but it had gotten to the point to where he was now using a magnifying glass in order to read.

And, contrary to what some people may have thought, Old Joe still liked to read books. In his earlier years, he'd been a voracious reader; however, two things were now standing in his way – his drinking and his eyesight.

Thus, if he wanted to read, it generally had to be in the morning, preferably within an hour or two after he'd first gotten up, when his mind and vision were as sharp as they would be for the rest of the day.

He would read books on anything historical, and had a special interest in the lives of artists – famous writers, painters, and musicians.

So not only did he like reading the books that had been written *by* Hemingway, Fitzgerald, and Bukowski, among others, but he also liked to read the stories that had been written *about* them – and how their drinking was viewed as being legendary.

You see, Old Joe had always subscribed to the theory that if you were crazy and poor, you were just crazy – however, if you were crazy and rich, you were eccentric. So, in other words – though by the same token – he believed that if you were a drunk who was able to write (especially to the degree of the aforementioned gentlemen) then your drinking would not only be perceived as being ok but it would actually be something that was celebrated.

At worse, you might be labeled as a "tortured soul" or a "mad genius."

"It all has to do with creativity," thought the old man.

Thus, having that innate ability to transfer one's thoughts so beautifully onto the written page would somehow exclude you from any societal rebuke.

Or if you possessed some other rare or extraordinary gift such as painting, or sculpting, or perhaps composing, or playing a musical instrument of any kind – then your drinking would once more be overlooked.

However, if all of these artistic talents were lacking and all you could do was drink – well, then you would simply be known as a drunk.

But like Old Joe used to say, "We're all drunks – in one way or another."

And perhaps that's why he found himself being so drawn to the stories of those extremely talented but often times troubled people.

Like Vincent Van Gogh.

How his brother Theo had shown him unwavering support throughout his entire life, both financially and emotionally, though he had never sold a single painting. His on again off again friendship with Gauguin – and whether that now infamous incident of him cutting off a piece of his own ear had indeed been a gesture of loyalty and was somehow intended as a gift.

Old Joe loved the idea that Van Gogh was *truly* both tortured and a genius, whose work was known by only a few before shooting himself, or so it's alleged, with no one having ever found the gun, and then dying at the tender age of 37 with his final words, "The sadness will last forever."

Every time Old Joe would read his story and then view his incredible works of art, he was in awe. Especially when considering the fact that one of his paintings had recently sold for 82.5 million.

Another of his favorite stories was that of Paul Cezanne, a remarkable painter who's considered by most to be one of the founders of post-impressionism and whose eyesight, after a lifetime of amazing works, had begun to fail. "Think of that," Old Joe would say to himself, "a painter going blind." And yet, he didn't quit.

As the story goes, even though his once incredible use of light had been reduced to a checkerboard of less-defined images and dramatic shadows, somehow his colors had become more defiant, with his earthy umbers and daunting ochers now something else entirely. Therefore, even at his advanced age, he was later recognized as having founded yet another artistic movement known as "post-impression-istic cubism."

"Absolutely brilliant," thought Old Joe.

Much like the story of the great composer Beethoven, who created his greatest works after he had gone almost completely deaf, by chopping the legs off of his piano and feeling the vibrations with his ear to the floor as he would strike each key.

"What word would you use to describe something like that?" thought Old Joe. *"Determination? Perseverance? Fortitude? Brilliance? Genius? Or is it some word that has yet to be discovered?"*

To him, stories like these were beyond fantastic.

They were indescribable.

And if the only hardship that *he* had to face in order to read them was having to use a magnifying glass, then so be it.

Although, years earlier, Old Joe had been watching a documentary on Paul Cezanne which depicted a sudden storm that the painter had been caught in one autumn afternoon with the narrator saying, *"After painting one day, he came back dying."*

Old Joe had always remembered these words, about the old man whose eyesight was failing, *"He came back dying."*

He now found them to be prophetic.

29.

It was late June and Old Joe was sitting out at the Tiki bar inside of Frosty's back patio. He had requisitioned the corner barstool and was getting a nice breeze coming in from off of the alleyway.

"Johnny B. Goode" was bartending and walked over to Old Joe and said, "Hey Joe, these two guys over here have a bet goin' and I said that you might be able to settle it for 'em – you know, being a history teacher and all – wanna give it a shot?"

"Sure," said Old Joe, "why not?"

People had begun to recognize Old Joe as an intelligent man not only because he seemed to know a lot of things but – as he had stated on more than one occasion – he'd also been a high school history teacher. So he'd been asked before to give his opinion on certain matters and to even settle a bar bet or two, but that was years ago, before he'd become a drunk and prior to the worldwide advent of cellphones. But, if these two guys were willing to accept his word as their final verdict, then he was willing to provide whatever assistance he could.

"Hey fellas," said Old Joe, "so what's the bet?"

"Hey, how ya' doin'? My name is Eric and this guy here is my idiot friend Jim and he doesn't think that Mexico and Central America are part of North America." And then Jim said, "No, wait a minute, that's not what I said exactly – I said that Mexico was part of *Central* America, so it's kinda like two bets in one, and this bartender here says that you used to know a lot of stuff so, who wins?"

"Well," said Old Joe, "I hate to tell you this Jim, but it looks like Eric is going to win those bets because both Mexico and Central America are part of North America – and though the two are sometimes referred to as one geographic region called 'Middle America,' they are indeed separate entities."

"Are you sure?" asked Jim. "Yeah," said Old Joe, "I'm pretty certain." "Well, screw this shit," he said, "I want to know for sure, rather than just asking some old dude sitting at a fucking Tiki bar. Come on Eric, stop screwin' around and just look it up on your phone – you know that I'd be lookin' if I hadn't lost mine, then we wouldn't be havin' this stupid argument." To which Eric replied, "Why should I? You probably wouldn't believe my phone either."

And then Old Joe said, "Well, now, hold on there a second Jim, if you give me the chance, I think that maybe I can prove it to you – all right?"

So Jim said, "Sure, whatever."

"Ok," said Old Joe, "most people would agree that we have seven continents on this planet – so do both of you fine young gentlemen concur with that premise?"

Each man nodded his head in approval and then Eric said, "Yeah, of course."

"And can we also agree that those seven continents are as follows: North America, South America, Europe, Asia, Africa, Australia, and Antarctica?"

Both men agreed.

"And can we also agree that excluding Antarctica only North America and South America are in the Western Hemisphere?"

And once more, both men were in agreement.

"And do both of you agree that Central America is *not* located within the continent of South America?"

The two men looked at each other and nodded, and then Jim said, "Yeah, that sounds about right."

And then Old Joe said, "Well, in that case, Eric wins – because all that's left is the continent that we happen to be sitting in right now and we call it 'North America.'"

"Shit!" said Jim.

Then Eric shouted, "Bravo! Hey barkeep, get the teacher here whatever he wants."

And that made the old man feel good.

He was happy.

30.

Every now and then, Old Joe would find himself thinking about his father and the conversations they used to have.

On this evening he was recalling the times when he would visit his parents each week for Sunday dinners, to talk to his mom about son and mother things, and to talk to his father about football or baseball, whichever was in season, and furnaces and tomatoes and automobiles. But mostly, they would talk about golf.

Oh, how his father loved that game.

Even in the dead of winter, Old Joe's dad would be as excited as a schoolboy when showing him the latest addition to the collection of clubs he kept in the basement where they would practice their swings, so effortlessly, before he was diagnosed with cancer.

Then came the day when his father called him on the phone. "I can't golf anymore," he said, "I can't make the swing," while deep down inside Old Joe was actually praying, *"of course you can, you're my father, you can do anything,"* as he began to foolishly recount a story that his father had first relayed to him about a wayward professional golfer (though at the time he couldn't remember his name) who, after seeking his father's advice, had once again found his game – by slowing everything down.

"His name was Bert Yancey," his father said, "but you don't understand," then he explained how he had lost his balance during a swing while attempting to play one last round with his friends. Old Joe tried to sound encouraging but, looking back, his father had called to tell him that he was dying.

And when he said, "Keep your eye on the ball" and "Remember to hit 'em straight," the old man now knew what his father had been trying to say.

But as he sat there at the bar at Mojito Bay motioning for Diago to bring him yet another beer, he realized that it was probably too late.

31.

Even though Old Joe had never been a fan of those big hotels being built on the island, at one time Put-In-Bay was the premier site of the largest hotel in the world.

It was called the Hotel Victory, a multi-towered Queen Anne-styled structure that was built with mules in only three years and then opened in 1892.

And like the "Perry's Victory and International Peace Memorial," which was completed in 1936, the Hotel Victory had been so named to memorialize Commodore Oliver Hazard Perry's stunning victory over the British during the War of 1812.

The main building measured 600 feet by 300 feet with 625 guest rooms along with an inner courtyard and was connected to another building which housed both the main dining hall and a smaller dining room. Together, the two dining areas could serve up to 1,200 guests at any one time.

There was an ice cream parlor, a barber shop, a greenhouse, wine cellars, a billiards room, and other extravagant furnishings which were estimated to have cost over one million dollars.

The massive structure included the following:

825 rooms

2,500 windows

1,700 doors

3,000 incandescent lights

20,000 yards of room carpeting

1 mile of hallway carpeting

16 acres of flooring

The hotel opened to great fanfare on July 29, 1892. However, by September 19 of that same year, it went into receivership. After closing and then reopening in August of 1893, it quickly closed again and stood empty for over a year and a half, and a sheriff's sale stripped the hotel of its once opulent furnishings in 1895.

Then, after being purchased for a mere $17,000, the hotel reopened to another wave of fanfare on July 20, 1896, with the major selling point being a 100 feet by 30 feet co-ed swimming pool.

But the hotel continued to go through periods of uncertainty with changing ownership until 1899, when that all changed with the introduction of Thomas McCreary as the new general manager. And like Diocletian from the days of the flagging Roman Empire, McCreary was keenly able to finally right the ship and – through his sheer will and forceful nature – the hotel became a success.

In 1907, at the height of its glory, McCreary commissioned a 13-foot-tall "Victory Statue" to be prominently displayed in the front of the hotel, an imposing figure of a winged goddess with a 7-foot-wide span. It was made of copper and bronze and perched beautifully atop a 9-foot-tall concrete pedestal. However, the skillful promoter and genius of showmanship responsible for this statue would die later that same year.

And like the revival period of the Roman Empire, the hotel's "glory days" were to be short-lived as once again there were closings and re-openings until that fateful year of 1919.

By that time there were only thirty guests staying there on the evening of August 14, when a sudden fire went roaring through those massive hallways signaling the end for the Hotel Victory.

Nowadays, only a few signposts still remain commemorating the last of the ruins – including the deteriorating pedestal and the dilapidated swimming pool – and though only a few people take the time to salute the flag by the cannon of "Perry's Memorial," fewer still come to witness the site of that once great hotel.

Maybe Old Joe had it right all along.

32.

Old Joe kept a journal.

But since it was no longer a daily endeavor, I guess one could say that it was more like a notebook – his three-ringed binder filled with some four hundred pages of which he would routinely change out, or rip up, and then replace with blank sheets. It was a place for him to write down his thoughts, poems, essays, and short stories – mostly having to do with history.

At one time, years earlier, he'd actually kicked around the idea of writing his own American History book, with lesson plans for teachers to use in their classrooms, but it never materialized.

Lately, however, he'd been working on a series of stories that he considered to be "the greatest in history" and though he was doing this primarily for his own enjoyment, it was also to see how much of the information he'd actually retained.

On this day, Old Joe flagged down "Eddie B." and ordered his fourth beer before opening his "journal" to the first blank page past

his working title of "History Teacher – A Few of My Favorite Stories."
As it was, he'd already completed the first three stories of his project:

1. The British Scientists Versus the German "Enigma" Machine

2. The Freak 1814 Tornado after the Burning Down
   of the White House

3. Abraham Lincoln and the Gettysburg Address

And he'd begun number "4."

"George Washington Crossing the Delaware River."

Old Joe loved "do or die" stories and for him, this one topped
them all. He'd always been impressed by the heroics of Washington
and considered him to be one of the greatest men to have ever lived.

A few days earlier, he'd written about the events which had ultimately led up to that most critical moment in history and the reasons
for the war known as "The American Revolution;" including "taxa-
tion without representation," the "Boston Massacre," and the "Tea
Act of 1773." And he'd also touched upon that little incident known
as the "Boston Tea Party," along with "Lexington and Concord" and
the "Battle of Bunker Hill."

So, this morning, he continued …

Thus the war had officially begun even prior to the "Declaration
of Independence," only now there was no turning back, and the
future of "The United States of America" was hanging in the balance.
But ever since that famous separation on July 4th of 1776 (although
the actual declaring of independence had taken place on July 2nd)
things had not gone well for Washington and his army. There were
some back then who thought the big Virginian to be a coward,

because his army was constantly running. But he knew that his army *was* "the revolution," and if captured all would be lost. Washington's army was made up of mostly farmers fighting the greatest army that the world had ever known and no one had given them "a snowball's chance in hell" except for the man himself who believed in miracles – so they ran.

They ran in September and October. Then they continued to run in November and even into mid-December, through New York and New Jersey and finally to the Delaware River in their latest of pell-mell retreats. Then, after crossing the river only a few steps ahead of the British, the two armies stood there and stared at each other from the opposing banks, with the Americans on the west being heckled by the British.

And for all intents and purposes, that was it. The war was over – and everyone seemed to know it.

That was because General Washington's army was made up of mostly one-year enlistments and come December 31st, given the impossible circumstances, virtually no one was going to re-up.

His men were starving, and freezing, with very little in the way of provisions, and hadn't had even a sniff of a victory in over a year; while the British ate well and rested in heated cabins, so he really couldn't blame his "gritty little handful" for simply waiting out those remaining days.

Even he, the great George Washington, when writing to his brother a week earlier had admitted, *"if every nerve is not strained to recruit the New Army with all possible expedition, I think the game is pretty near up."*

But then, when he needed it most, at that very moment in history when it looked for certain that the fledgling United States of America was no more, the man who believed in miracles made one happen.

He devised a plan.

A few days before Christmas, he called his officers into his tent. Most of them thought that the old man was going to give them a toast for having done the best that they could and to simply say, "Oh well, I guess that it wasn't in the cards," but nothing could've been further from the truth. Instead, Washington gave the order, "Attack!"

Now mind you, this is an army that hadn't come close to a victory in well over a year, and one that had never defeated the British in open battlefield or in hand to hand combat. Nonetheless, Washington said, "Come Christmas Eve, we go." Some of his officers began to whisper behind his back, still others even hinted at mutiny, after all, the men were starving and the river was frozen – and Trenton was nine long miles away.

The plan was to set out in rows of three and to reach the other side of the river by sometime around two in the morning, and then to hike the nine miles eastward and attack the Hessians before sunrise.

However, things went bad from the start. Of the three rows that had set out to cross the river, one never really got started, and another went only part way, so only Washington's boat was able to manage the ice flow and make it all the way to the other side. But, by the time all of his men were able to follow his path and get to the other side, they'd fallen terribly behind schedule. The men were exhausted and their powder was wet – and the sun was beginning to rise.

When informed about the wet gun powder, Washington said, "Tell the men to attach the bayonets," and when asked if the delay had ruined their element of surprise he said, "We march."

The men without shoes were becoming frost-bitten while others began succumbing to the cold, but as a few laid themselves down to never rise again the rest of the army marched on.

And by the time they reached Trenton, though the sun was well up in the sky, there was complete surprise after all – for just as Washington had planned, the Hessians were still drunk from their Christmas Eve revelry.

As the battle ensued there was fierce hand to hand combat but the fighting was over in less than an hour, and when the smoke had cleared and the mayhem was over it was the Americans who stood victorious.

The casualties from the battle were as follows:
Americans – 4 wounded; 0 dead
Hessians – 100 wounded; 20 dead; 1,000 captured

And now the Americans had food, blankets, boots, and weapons along with the much needed ammunition – but, even though his officers were begging him to pause and to give the men time to rest, Washington knew that word would get out and that they had to make it back to safety across the river. So, at this point, we can only imagine the soldiers' absolute exhaustion and how for no other man would they have listened. Yet, they once again took the great man's orders and marched those nine grueling miles back and then re-crossed the river.

Then, finally, they could rest – and eat!

And miraculously, in one daring and fell swoop, George Washington had saved both the revolution and The United States of America.

After this humiliating defeat, having been caught literally with their pants down, the British stationed troops directly across the river to make sure that it wouldn't happen again.

A few nights later, Washington had his men back away slowly from their campfires and slip quietly into the darkness – they marched north for several miles before once more crossing the river – and then, a couple days after that, they attacked Princeton.

Old Joe put down his pen and stretched out his arms before standing and ordering another beer. Writing that story had taken a lot out of him, and it was already half-past noon. But then he thought, *"I can write one more."*

So after "Eddie B." had delivered yet another cold one, the old man picked up his pen and wrote down the number "5."

"The Polish Cavalry Versus the German 76th Panzer Division."

Being of Polish descent, Old Joe had always had a soft spot in his heart for this story. He remembered Sister Agnes Marie telling his seventh grade class all about it, how the Polish Cavalry at the onset of World War II had attacked the German tanks with only their horses and swords. His classmates all laughed and said, "Boy, were they stupid," but not Old Joe. He thought they were brave. In fact, he thought that it was one of the greatest stories that he had ever heard.

Though now he thought, *"Who's to say?"* Maybe there is a fine line between bravery and stupidity, depending on which side of history you happen to be standing – the victorious or the vanquished.

Then again, maybe his classmates were all too young to realize that one day, we all must perish – even them. Even the members of the German 76th Panzer Division. So, to him, it begged the question, *"How would you rather go out?"* Like a Polish soldier, while charging on horseback versus a Nazi tank and as you're staring into the face of death, or after having spent your final days in some nursing home?

Either way, that story, along with the others, would have to wait for another day.

Old Joe was tired. More tired than he had realized.

So he put the pen inside of his notebook, closed the cover, and got up to leave. He reached into his pocket and pulled-out three twenty dollar bills to cover whatever his cost may've been and to leave a tip. Then he waved good-bye to Eddie – or at least put his left hand in the air to indicate that he was leaving– and headed for Frosty's. However, about a quarter of the way down Delaware Avenue, he turned around and started walking back in the other direction toward his motel room.

He needed to take a nap.

33.

By the time Old Joe had awakened, the clock read 5:32 and he thought, *"Is it morning or afternoon?"* As it turned out, it was still afternoon, but he had been asleep for some four hours and had changed his routine for the day. So at first he thought, *"I'll take a quick shower and head on over to The Roundhouse."* But then he thought, *"Nah, I'll sleep a little more and then go down to The Boathouse and see Sarita."*

However, he was still very tired and just didn't feel right and thought, *"Screw it – I'll just pick-up a six-pack and stay in tonight and watch a game."* So then, after staying in bed for a few more hours, he got up, splashed some cold water on his face, and headed out the door. He walked over to the carry-out which was less than a block away and picked up a six-pack of Coors Light bottles. Then he put those back and decided to get a twelve-pack instead.

And while he was waiting to check out, he noticed a DVD of the movie *"Casablanca"* on one of those little round carousels standing next to the counter – and affixed to the wrapper was an orange sticker. *"Who in the hell marks down Casablanca?"* he thought, and maybe for that reason alone he bought it – along with the beer.

The TV in his room had one of those built-in DVD players with a slot on the side through which to slide the disc, but Old Joe had never used one before and he was hoping that he would be able to get it to work as he was walking back to the motel.

He opened a beer and put the rest in the fridge then sat down on his bed to watch this all-time classic. He remembered when he was twelve and was viewing it for the first time and how he couldn't believe that *Rick* was letting *Ilsa* walk away. And yet, with each excruciating step through that moonlit fog, as if it were some kind of arbitrary measure between right and wrong, their distance grew until finally – she was gone.

And years later, while watching it again, as Rick's pistol was pointing straight at the heart of Major Strasser, with his same stony-faced determination that Old Joe had always admired, he realized that he was older than Bogart had been and wondered how that was possible.

Then tonight, while sitting on his bed in that motel room, Old Joe found it rather hard to believe that he was once more following that winding arrow on that marvelous map, through Europe and Africa and to a place called *Casablanca,* just so he could view the world again in black and white.

He didn't go out that night.

And he never did turn on the game.

34.

Old Joe was sitting on the wooden bench at the front of The Boathouse. Sarita was at the bar getting him a beer. When she came back, she smiled and said, "Here you go Papa," to which he responded, "Thanks honey," then he gave her a ten and said, "keep the change." He'd already been there for a few hours so Sarita asked, "Are you going to be here much longer?"

"Why?" he asked. "Are you trying to get rid of me or somethin'?" And Sarita said, "Oh no Papa, nothing like that, I was just seeing if you were going to be needing anything – so, where is it that you go when you leave here anyway?" And Old Joe said, "Well, I usually just go over to the Mojito to see my buddy Diago," and then he noticed a rather quizzical look on her face so he added, "I would stay here longer except, I might pass out from your beauty."

And then she said, "Oh, just stop it now old man, or I might actually begin to believe you – you know?" "Well you can go right ahead and believe me then," he said, "because it's true." "Whatever," said Sarita with a little smile on her face, and she started shaking her head as she was walking away but then turned slightly and added,

"I'll bet you were a pistol when you were younger – weren't you?" Then Old Joe shouted behind her, "I was a sweetheart," and he could see her starting to laugh as she went to wait on the other customers.

Then Old Joe sat on the bench drinking his beer and thinking about Sarita, with the voices of "Eddie B." and Diago ringing in his ears. And now he was starting to think that maybe they were right, that he didn't just like this girl, but that he was in love with her. *"Whatever in the hell that is,"* he thought.

Although, at the very least, he was certain that he enjoyed her company, perhaps more than anyone's company that he could remember, and for a brief moment he even entertained the thought of asking her to go out with him. *"Maybe when she gets off work,"* he thought. But, on a small island around 2:30 in the morning, what he'd really be asking her to do is to come home with him – and the problem wasn't so much that she would say "no," the problem was that she might actually say "yes."

And though as a younger man he would've jumped at the chance to spend the night with a beautiful woman like Sarita, he was now older and wiser and was thinking more about what would happen the next day. Because the one thing that he wanted more than anything else was for Sarita and him to remain friends. So, instead of hanging around that night, he decided that it would be best to just get her attention from across the room – by once again putting his hand in the air as if to say "goodnight" – and simply leave in her good graces. Then, tomorrow, he could come back and take things from there. And that's exactly what he did.

But as he crossed Hartford Avenue, he began to immediately question his decision. However, he didn't have that sick feeling in the pit of his stomach – the kind he would usually get after having made a mistake or after having done something that he knew to be wrong – which he took to be a good sign.

And then while walking through the park he looked over toward the neon lights on Delaware Avenue and even though they seemed blurry coming through his old and tired eyes he thought, *"But they're still beautiful, so that's ok,"* as he continued along feeling somewhat chivalrous.

Then he heard some laughter coming from the boats on the bay. It was young laughter, a little farther down the line, and as he looked out into the darkness a smile came to his face and in a soft voice he said to himself, "That used to be me."

35.

Old Joe stepped up to the jukebox and clanked down a few quarters.

He knew the numbers by heart.

One-Three-Zero-Seven.

One-Three-One-One.

Five-Four-Zero-Two.

A couple of Sinatra songs and a Waylon and Willie classic.

He loved a good jukebox. Give him a barstool, a cold beer, and a jukebox, and Old Joe would be as happy as a pig in shit.

Boomp ba-boom, boomp ba-boom, boomp ba-boom, boomp ba-boom,

Fly me to the moon, da da daaa da da da da ...

Then the tremendously full and rich sound of the fabulous Count Basie Orchestra began to flood into those adjoining rooms of that little bar and pizzeria along with the incredibly distinctive voice of "ol' blue eyes" telling the timeless story of how a simple kiss from that one special lady – or even the mere act of holding her hand – can send a man into orbit.

It was the Fourth of July and there were just too damned many people on the island – that is, for Old Joe's liking. By ten in the morning he could almost feel the whole place beginning to tilt.

But the old man had a plan. He knew that by 10:30, on this day anyway, things were going to be a challenge. So he decided to start early, per usual, for the explicit purpose of avoiding the crowds, which was one of the reasons why he liked to drink in the morning in the first place – that, and the fact that he was an alcoholic.

And though he'd never been a fan of the big hotels with those "stupid-ass" swim-up bars they added a few years back, there was one thing about them that he did like – on days such as this, they served a purpose. Because even though these attractions did indeed bring more people to the island, *a lot* more people, they also gave those extra tourists *other* places to go and drew them away from Delaware Avenue. And Old Joe, being a traditionalist, usually hung around the downtown bars. Oh sure, he would occasionally wander off, but he could tell which side of his bread was buttered and on days like this he knew a secret: Frosty's Bar.

Frosty's had always been one of his "core four," and that's where he was again today, listening to the jukebox.

His next selection was the song "Summer Wind," a little 1965 gem written by four heavyweights of their day – Henry Mayer, Hans Bradtke, Johnny Mercer and Heinz Meier – and once again that one of a kind voice of Sinatra began to regale those listening with the story of a man losing his love to, of all things, the wind. Though, not to just any wind, not to the autumn wind or even to those dreaded winter winds, but rather to that damned old summer wind.

Now it should go without saying that Old Joe's "core four" had always been (in no particular order) the Beer Barrel, The Roundhouse, The Boathouse, and Frosty's.

And just so there's no misunderstanding, there were going to be an awful lot of people at *all* of these establishments – especially on the Fourth of July. However, at Frosty's, you could still get a seat at the bar and listen to the jukebox as if it were a regular weekday.

That's because most of the Fourth of July crowd came to the Frosty's *restaurant* section to get a slice or two of their world famous pizza, but then bypassed the bar area for the more "glitzy" attractions. And I guess we have to give it to the old coot because, by two o'clock in the afternoon, his plan was working with things still looking (*and sounding*) pretty good as his third choice began to play on the juke-box – a song written in 1975 by the husband and wife team of Ed and Patsy Bruce originally titled "Mammas Don't Let Your Babies Grow Up To Be Guitar Players." However, after the words "guitar players" were replaced with the word "cowboys" and the superstar country duo of Waylon Jennings and Willie Nelson decided to give the song a whirl of their own a couple of years later well, the rest as they say is history.

Mammas don't let your babies grow up to be cowboys ...

36.

The craziness of July 4th had passed and things on the island had pretty much gotten back to normal – except, that is, for Old Joe. He decided to do something a little different this morning.

After leaving the Beer Barrel he skipped going to Frosty's and rented a golf cart instead so that he could take a ride around the island. These vehicles were by far the most popular mode of transportation at Put-In-Bay and were an especially nice way to get around on those hot and sticky days such as this.

There's a dozen or so rental shops on the island though Old Joe went to the one on Delaware Avenue, of course, since it sits directly in between Frosty's and the Beer Barrel. Then he chose a two-seater, hopped in, and away he went. He pulled onto Delaware heading east and then proceeded down to Toledo Avenue where he turned left and drove the few hundred feet to Bayview. There he turned right and headed out to "Perry's Victory Memorial" and beyond, going another mile or so up the road to the farthest northeastern point on the island. He got out of his golf cart for a bit and stood on the rocks overlooking Lake Erie before walking a little ways up a dirt road that ran adjacent to the most perfect vineyard that you would ever want to see. Then, as he continued along, he happened upon this wonderful trail created by the locals. It wound its way through a thorny thicket sitting on the lake's edge and came complete with secret passageways and dead ends, hand-painted signs with arrows, old wooden benches made out of rough-hewn branches and randomly placed tombstones and small hidden placards for the dead.

The place was pure magic and it had a definite effect upon the old man.

So after staying for much longer than he had originally planned, he got back in his golf cart and returned the same way from which he'd came – since that was the only way he could go – down State Route 357 and past the memorial once again. But this time, upon returning to the corner of Delaware and Toledo, he kept going. He headed south on Langram Road for approximately two miles (with the island itself being only 4 miles long and about 2 miles wide) before turning right onto Meechen and going down another half-mile or so to Catawba Avenue and proceeded directly into South Bass Island State Park.

Then after driving through the trailer park, Old Joe got out of his golf cart and walked over to the ruins of the "Hotel Victory," which at one time had been the largest hotel in the world.

He looked around the old swimming pool, which seemed miniscule by today's standards, and stood beside the pedestal that once held the "Victory Statue," that amazing 13-foot-tall winged goddess made of copper and bronze. For whatever reason, Old Joe had always loved to walk amongst the ruins of old buildings, to stand on that exact spot of earth where others had been, in places once filled with happiness and laughter – but now fraught with feelings of sadness and despair. And there were times, he would say, in places such as this, when he could almost feel someone's presence. But Old Joe didn't mind, in fact, he would often joke that it was simply his guardian angel watching over him.

So after he'd finished surveying the ruins, he traveled the short distance over to "Joe's Bar" to have a cold one. "Joe's" was a great bar, a true classic, located on Catawba Avenue just a stone's throw away from the state park. It had that "old time" feel that simply can't be manufactured, with a certain comfortable and relaxing atmosphere that put you instantly at ease, as if you were visiting a neighbor's cottage. And every time he was there Old Joe would say to himself, "Why don't I come here more often?" But that was simply an excuse, for he knew that he could've gone there whenever he wanted.

And when he'd finished wetting his whistle a time or two, with a couple Coors Light and a Bloody Mary that would've given "Eddie B." a run for his money, he got back in his golf cart and went taking off as fast as it would go down Catawba, as he began heading back toward the downtown bars. He passed the "Heineman Winery" and then the "Goat Soup and Whiskey" and then the "Reel Bar" (to name but a few places) before finally approaching Hooligan's and Mojito Bay. Then he eased his foot off the "gas" and continued to slow down until he was barely puttering along and turned right onto Delaware Avenue.

He was home.

37.

It was a Friday morning at the Beer Barrel and Old Joe had an eleven o'clock appointment with "Big Sal." Unlike most bookies, "Big Sal" gave permission for some of his *special* clients to run a weekly tab, so they would usually meet before the weekend to settle the score.

Old Joe was waiting at the bar for Sal when "Eddie B." walked up and said, "So what are you working on now Old Joe, writing that 'Great American Novel' again?"

"No, not quite kid," said Old Joe, "I'm just checking to see how close I am to shitting myself."

"Come again?"

"Oh, never mind, I'm just kidding – I'm doing a crossword puzzle."

"Looks like fun," quipped Eddie, "boy, you're just a real rebel these days, you know that?"

"Well, trust me," said the old man, "one of these days you'll be doing crosswords too."

"Time waits for no man, hey Joe?"

"That's right Eddie – that's exactly correct."

And just as the young bartender was walking away, "Big Sal" showed up and sat down in a barstool next to him.

"Hey old man," said Sal, "how's it hangin'?"

And Old Joe replied, "Oh, I'd say medium-soft – how 'bout you?"

"It's a long story," said Sal. Then he continued, "Hey, you ain't been doin' so good, you're down fifteen."

"Yeah, I know, no big deal – here you go."

Then Old Joe handed him an envelope that he'd previously prepared filled with fifteen crisp one hundred dollar bills. Sal took a quick look inside the envelope and said, "You want anything tonight?" "Sure," said Old Joe, "give me two large on Houston," then Sal looked at him and said, "Anything else?"

"Nah, I think that's it – you can't go wrong with Verlander."

"Ok," said Sal, "you got it."

So the big man lifted himself up from his seat and with his meat-hook of a right hand shook with Old Joe, and then as he was leaving he glanced back and said, "Hang loose old man."

And Old Joe replied, "You know it kid."

38.

It didn't happen very often, but Old Joe was "beered-out."

And when it did happen, it was usually only for that day – or evening, in this case. But, for the moment, he'd had his fill. And as he was walking into Mojito Bay he knew that a couple of Diago's "change of pace" drinks were definitely an option, though what he really had a taste for was a Bloody Mary. However, as good of a bartender as Diago was, those were not his specialty.

His mastery was more evident in those "fruity-rum" drinks, so Old Joe would simply have to wait 'til morning if he wanted one of "Eddie B's" famous Bloody Marys.

"After all," he thought, *"beggars can't be choosers."*

His buddy Diago saw him coming, so he got out the old man's personal barstool that he always kept behind the bar and plopped it down into the sand while shouting, "What'll it be my fine sir?"

"Well young man," said Old Joe as he was walking up, "believe it or not, I think that I'm gonna stay away from beer this evening – so what do you recommend?"

"That depends," said Diago, "are you thinking whiskey? Rum? Tequila? Vodka? All of the above?"

"Tell you what," said Old Joe, "do you have any Southern Comfort?"

"Why, yes sir, we do."

"And would you happen to have any Vernors on hand?"

"Um, let me check real quick," said Diago, as he bent down to look in one of the mini-fridges underneath the bar countertop, then he came back up and said, "Yep, we've got a couple cans."

"Outstanding," said Old Joe, "I'll take that half-and-half in the tallest glass you got with some ice – and then we'll move on from there."

"Ok," said Diago, "you got it – sounds like you're gonna make me earn my money tonight."

"Damn straight," said Old Joe.

And so he sat there and watched Diago work the bar while finishing his Southern Comfort and Vernors.

And then he ordered another.

But, after that, he decided to move on to something else.

Diago asked, "So are we stickin' with whiskey or are we gonna get a little crazy here and mix 'em up?"

"Let's mix 'em up," said Old Joe, "tell ya' what – how 'bout a Long Island?"

"Sounds good," said Diago, "comin' right up." Then he said, "Boy, if you wanted to mix things up this is sure the right drink for that – so, did you see Sarita tonight?"

"Yeah, I saw her for a little bit – but she was pretty busy, so it was mostly small talk."

"Uh-oh, I hope you're not losin' your touch."

"Don't worry about me kid, I can hold up my end just fine."

"All right," said Diago, "as long as you're still movin' the ball down the field."

"I told ya' buddy, I used to play running back – so I'm ok."

"That's good to know," said Diago, "just checking."

This was all bullshit, of course, nothing more than "guy talk" between friends. The truth was, Old Joe liked things just the way they were with Sarita, and he now felt closer to her than ever before.

"Here's your drink," said Diago, "let me know when you need a refill."

"Thanks," said Old Joe, and then after waiting a couple seconds for Diago to walk away he shouted, "I'll send up a flare," because he knew that would put a smile on the young man's face.

So then, as he was sitting there, drinking his Long Island Iced Tea and watching the other patrons swaying back and forth on their rope swing chairs, he started thinking once more about Sarita and how things might've been different if he were younger.

"How about that," he thought, *"an actual woman friend."*

"Will wonders never cease?"

39.

Old Joe was very drunk. He was walking back to his motel room at two in the morning wearing a medal of St. Jude around his neck. And now he was reaching inside of his shirt to grasp it, first with his index finger and then with his thumb, and once he had placed it between the two, he began to rub.

It had been a gift from his grandmother on the day of his high school graduation and he'd worn it almost every day throughout at least his mid-twenties. Then one day, after taking it off, he simply stopped wearing it.

And after forty years or so, or for what had seemed like forever, it had somehow found its way into the bottom of Old Joe's leather toiletry bag where it had remained lying alongside a spare tooth-brush, a stick of deodorant, and a couple of Band-Aids.

But then, a few weeks back, he was having trouble falling asleep, so he decided to turn on the TV for a little while and after flipping through the stations came upon an old episode of "Unsolved Mysteries."

It was about a 7 year-old boy living in Philadelphia in 1982. He'd fallen into a coma and the doctors had said that his chances were slim. However, after receiving a holy medal from one of his family members, he had not only miraculously awakened, but had started telling people about this strange little boy who had visited him in the hospital.

He said that the little boy was very kind, but that he wore odd clothes and didn't seem to have come from this time or place.

Several nurses had reported seeing this little boy in the hallways, but no one had questioned him as to why he was there. Then a few days later, just before Christmas, the "miracle child" (as he was being called) was released from the hospital after having made a full recovery.

The child's name was Chucky McGivern.

And then a week or so later, when his family was visiting a local church to offer prayers of thanks, he recognized a painting of that strange little boy who had visited him while he'd been in his coma. Only, it was a portrait of Saint John Neumann as a child – the same saint whose likeness was on the holy medal that Chucky had been given in the hospital.

And Saint John Neumann had died in 1860.

After seeing this, Old Joe had immediately gotten out of bed and went looking to retrieve that medal of St. Jude from the bottom of his toiletry bag, the same medal that his grandmother had given him so many years ago, and placed it back around his neck.

St. Jude is the patron saint of lost causes.

He'd been wearing it ever since.

40.

It was another hot July afternoon, and Old Joe was once again sitting at the Tiki bar on the back patio at Frosty's.

He'd struck-up a conversation with a young couple wearing Ray-Ban sunglasses and flashing perfect smiles named Tom and Katie. He was a computer salesman and she was a high school English teacher and when Old Joe told her that he had once been a teacher himself, they had an instant connection.

"Were you a good teacher?" she asked. "I'd like to think so," said Old Joe, "I mean the kids liked me and they seemed to learn a few things, so I guess that kind of speaks for itself."

"But, why did they like you?" she asked again.

"What do you mean?"

"Well, was it that you were an easy grader or did you let them get away with things – or did you just do something that they really seemed to enjoy?" Then Tom said, "For gosh sakes honey, would you let the man breathe – we're supposed to be here having fun."

Then Old Joe said, "No, that's ok Tom, I don't mind – I was once a young teacher myself." And then he looked at Katie square in her Ray-Bans and said, "This might be hard for you to believe looking at me now, but when I was younger, I actually had a really good rapport with my students – so, I hope that they liked me for the simple fact that I was a pretty good teacher."

Then Katie said, "Oh shit, I'm sorry, I'm making you defensive – my husband's right, sometimes I have a big mouth."

And Old Joe replied, "No, honestly, there's no offense taken, I totally understand – all teachers want to be well-liked." And then he asked, "Are you well-liked?" And Katie said, "Well, I don't want to steal your answer but, like you, I'd like to think so – but you know what," she quickly added, "If I'm really being honest with myself, they probably don't like me as much as I think they do."

"Well," Old Joe said with a laugh, "I guess that makes you normal then, doesn't it?" Then Katie laughed, which was more like a sigh of relief, and Tom said, "Anybody need anything? I'm buyin'."

To which Katie answered, "Sure, I'd love another," and Old Joe said, "Why thank you kind sir, I'll have a Coors Light."

Then Katie mentioned how hot it was, and Tom said that they'd been at The Sand Bar all day yesterday, but Katie's mind returned to teaching and she asked Old Joe, "So, what did you do that the kids liked?" And he said, "Well, that's been a few years ago now but, I remember that I gave them a lot of quizzes."

"Quizzes?" asked Katie.

"Oh yeah," he said, "about every other day or so – to make sure that they kept up with their reading."

"And your students liked that?"

"Well," he added, "I would try to make the quizzes fun, you know, by asking extra-credit questions and things like that."

Then in a sarcastic tone Katie said, "Wow – that sounds like a real blast."

"Actually," said Old Joe, "it was – because the extra-credit questions were mostly trivia. You know, pop culture stuff, nothing to do with the subject matter – or at least that's what the kids thought."

"What do you mean?' asked Katie, "give me an example."

And then Tom said, "Yeah, now you've even got me a little curious."

"Ok," said Old Joe, "like I said, I would try to do a few things that were fun and that would help the students grades a little, but I also wanted them to learn the material so, let's say that I gave you a quiz, fifteen questions, one point a piece, for a total of fifteen points. Then, I would have you and your classmates trade papers and we would grade them in class – and that's when I would obviously reread all of the questions *along* with the answers, ok?

But let's say that you didn't do your reading homework last night, and you only got nine questions right – now, nine out of fifteen is sixty per cent and in most schools that's an 'F' or maybe a 'D-'.

So, to help your grade a little, but more importantly to help you *learn*, I'd say to the class, 'Ok, anyone with a ten or below crumple up your papers and throw them away' – and then I would hold up the waste basket so that you and your classmates could have a little fun trying to make baskets while at the same time throwing some paper wads at the teacher.

Then I would say, 'All right, take out another sheet of paper,' and I would give them that very same quiz again."

"You're kidding," said Katie. "Isn't that cheating?"

"What cheating?" asked Old Joe. "It's a quiz – besides, they're *learning* the information. And isn't that what it's all about?" "Ok," said Katie, "but where do the trivia questions come in?" "I'm glad you asked," said Old Joe. "So either on the first or second quiz, or sometimes both, I would ask them an extra-credit question or two and would tell them that they were 'pure gravy,' which meant that they were 'extra-credit' and couldn't hurt anyone's grade."

Katie furrowed her brow and gave Old Joe a puzzled look.

"Ok," he said, "I can see that we need another example. Let's say that on your first quiz you still got your nine out of fifteen, but during that first quiz I had asked you and your class two extra-credit questions. Something like, 'Number sixteen – What is the name of Bart Simpson's best friend?' So the answer of course would be 'Milhouse' – right? Then I would say, 'Number seventeen – The 37th president of the United States was a man named Richard M. Nixon, so what did the 'M' stand for? Or, in other words, what was his middle name?' And, once again, his middle name was 'Milhous,' only spelled without the 'e' at the end."

"No way," said Tom, "you actually did that?"

"Sure did," said Old Joe, "all the time."

"But how did you do the grading?" asked Katie.

"That's an outstanding question young lady. First of all, I would only count the number correct, never how many were missed – that's important. Students should always be graded on what they know, not what they don't know."

"Hold on a second," said Katie, "I think it's time for another example."

"Ok," said Old Joe, "If you had gotten your nine out of fifteen right on the quiz, but you also answered the two extra credit questions correctly, your grade would've then become an eleven – so it helped you, right? However, extra credit could never *hurt* someone's grade, nor should it – so if someone else got a fourteen out of fifteen, but missed both extra credit questions, there grade would remain a fourteen."

"You know what Joe," said Katie, "that's not bad – as a matter of fact, that's rather brilliant."

"And you did this all the time?"

"Yep, at least once or twice a week."

"But wouldn't you need a lot of extra credit questions for that, I mean – where did you get them from?"

"From everywhere," said Old Joe.

"Everywhere?"

"Yeah, sure – I used to play this other game with my students called 'The Conference Game,' where they separated into teams and answered various history questions; anyway, one of the categories that they could choose from was called the 'Grab Bag.' Now, with this category, they never knew what they would get, but a lot of the questions dealt with pop culture and some other things that I had just thrown in there over the years – so I had literally hundreds of questions."

"Hundreds?" asked Katie. "Really?"

"Oh yeah," said Old Joe, "I can still remember a lot of 'em – would you like to hear some?"

"Sure," answered Katie.

"Ok," said Old Joe, "Tell ya' what, if you and your old man here are up for it, I'll just throw out a question and if either one of you knows the answer just go ahead and shout it – ok?"

They both nodded their heads and Tom said, "Yeah, sure, why not?"

"All right then," said Old Joe, "we'll start with 'Famous Dogs.' Ready? What was the name of the dog in the comic strip 'Peanuts?'"

"Snoopy," shouted Katie.

"Correct, very good," said Old Joe, "one point for you."

Then he asked, "How 'bout 'The Grinch?'"

And after a moment Katie asked, "What do you mean 'The Grinch?'"

"You know," said Old Joe, "Dr. Seuss – 'The Grinch Who Stole Christmas' – what was the dog's name?"

"Oh my God," said Katie, "I know this."

"I do too," said Tom.

But after a few seconds Old Joe said, "The dog's name was Max."

"Oh, I knew that," said a frustrated Katie.

"Well," said Old Joe, "there *is* a time limit you know – let's make it five seconds, ok?"

To which both of them nodded and said, "Sure, ok."

"All right," said Old Joe, "we're gonna speed things up now so, if you know the answer, just shout it out. If you don't, then I'll let both of you know in about five seconds – ok? All set?"

"Rapid fire," said the old man, "here we go."

Then Old Joe began peppering the young couple with trivia from days gone by, providing Tom and Katie with both the questions *and* the answers if so needed.

Beginning, of course, with "Famous Dogs."

The old man asked, "What was the name of the dog in 'Garfield?' *Odie;* 'The Flintstones?' *Dino;* 'The Jetsons?' *Astro;* 'The Simpsons?' *Santa's little helper.*"

"Ok," said Old Joe, "now it's time for 'Name the President.'" Then he continued. "Who was – the first president? *Washington;* The second? *Adams;* The third? *Jefferson;* The fourth? *Madison;* The fifth? *Monroe;* The seventh? *Jackson;* The sixteenth? *Lincoln;* The thirty-third? *Truman;* The thirty-fifth? *Kennedy;* The thirty-seventh? *Nixon.*"

Then Old Joe asked, "Have you guys had enough – or do you want more?"

"Are you kidding?" asked Katie. "Is that all you got?"

"Bring it," said Tom.

"Ok," said Old Joe, "you asked for it – now we're going to do 'Winnie the Pooh' for five hundred; what's the name of the little boy? *Christopher Robbin;* The tiger? *Tigger;* The rabbit? *Rabbit;* The kanga-roo? *Kanga;* The baby kangaroo? *Roo;* The pig? *Piglet.*"

"Ha, ha," said Katy, "I got every one of those – bang! In your face Tom. I'm a 'Winnie the Pooh' expert."

Then she shouted, "Next!"

"All right," said Old Joe, "let's give Tom a fighting chance here. How about 'Famous Football Nicknames' for two hundred – here we go; which team was known as The 'Orange Crush?' *Broncos;* The 'Doomsday Defense?' *Cowboys;* The 'Purple People-Eaters?' *Vikings;* The 'Fearsome Foursome?' *Rams;* The 'Monsters of the Midway?' *Bears.*"

"Ha, ha," said Katie again, while pointing at Tom, "I'm still kickin' your ass!"

"You only knew one of those," said Tom.

"So," she retorted, "you didn't know any."

Then Old Joe interrupted their little tete-a-tete and said, "Ok, now baseball names. I'll give you the nickname and you give me the player. Ready? The 'Say Hey Kid?' *Willie Mays;* The 'Sultan of Swat?' *Babe Ruth;* The 'Georgia Peach?' *Ty Cobb;* 'Joltin' Joe?' *Joe DiMaggio;* The 'Big Hurt?' *Frank Thomas.*"

"Whew," said Old Joe, "I'm getting tired – I think I need a beer."

"Ok," said Katie, "I'll tell ya' what – if you do a few more cartoons, I'll buy ya' one."

"All right," said Old Joe, "We'll do some cartoon association questions and then that's it – are you ready?"

"Dr. Bruce Bannon? *The Incredible Hulk;* The name of George Jetson's son? *Elroy;* Clark Kent? *Superman;* The name of the skunk in 'Bambi?' *Flower;* The name of Scooby-Doo's van? *The Mystery*

Machine; Tonto? *The Lone Ranger;* Pokey the horse? *Gumby;* The name of the little girl in the Grinch? *Cindy Lou Who;* Kato? *The Green Hornet."*

"Aw, come on," said Katie, "freaking Kato? How are we supposed to know that?"

"Ok," said Old Joe, "last one – and if either one of you gets this, I'll be very impressed." Then he asked, "Who is 'The Number One Super Guy?'"

And then he waited for a few seconds, but they were completely stumped.

"What are you talking about?" asked Tom.

"Oh come on," said a sarcastic Old Joe, "everyone knows this."

Then he yelled out, "It's *Hong Kong Phooey!*"

"Oh my God," said Katie again, "I've never even heard of that before."

"Well," said Old Joe, "that's what's wrong with you millennials."

Then he asked, "So how do you think you guys did, anyway – what were your grades?"

"'F' for me," said Tom, and then Katie said, "I'd probably say that I got somewhere around a 'B.'" "Oh bullshit," said Tom, then Old Joe laughed and said, "Hey, for first-timers, you both did very well."

Then the old man looked at Katie and said, "By the way, I'll take that Coors Light now."

She smiled and said, "You got it."

41.

On another typical weekday, somewhere around mid-afternoon, Old Joe was once again walking down to that beautiful, old, red building known as The Roundhouse when he heard some strange, yet familiar music.

It was Jerry Reed's old tune, "East Bound and Down," from the movie "Smokey and the Bandit." He had always loved this song but had never heard it being played by a live band before – let alone here.

After walking inside he immediately looked toward the front to see just "who" the band might be, but the place was packed per usual and he couldn't find a banner of any kind. Then he spotted "little Becky" and held up a finger to indicate that he was ready for a cold one and pointed to where he would be standing. So he fought his way through the crowd the best he could while trying to make it to the last row of the supposed dance floor, though from what he could see no one was really "dancing" per se, rather everyone was just drinking and stomping their feet and having a good time.

And as the band continued to play that raucous song about a couple of buddies rollin' through the south and crossing state lines to pick up some illegal beer, total strangers began putting their arms around Old Joe and he began putting his arms around them, and while everyone was joining along and singing to the music he thought to himself, *"Where else in the world are people partying to 'East Bound and Down' right now – seriously?"* But then he thought, *"Oh no, that's something like that 'silly-ass' Nicholas would think in that book that Sarita gave me to read – holy shit! Maybe she's right – maybe I am just like that goofy bastard."*

However, even this horrifying revelation couldn't dampen his spirits as the people kept singing and the music played on,

East bound and down, ba dom bom bom bom ba dom – ba dom, ba dom, ba dom bom bom ba dom …

Then "little Becky" came up with his beer and he gave her a crisp twenty and said, "Keep it honey," and she gave him a quick hug and a little "sugar on the jaw."

So he took a big swig of his beer and then another one after that, and then another one after that, and he was off and runnin' just like the "Bandit."

And that old "Roundhouse magic" was back.

"Alive and well," thought Old Joe, *"alive and well."*

42.

Old Joe had another dream last night.

Only, this one began more like a memory.

He was a child, about ten years old, playing in his grandparent's backyard. Everything was there, just as it had been, all laid out in living color. The old garage with the warped beams, the little two-seat swing where he used to sway back and forth with his grandma, the pastel Virgin Mary surrounded by flowers, the fire-eaten oil barrel behind the garage, and the apple tree, of course, the center-piece of grandpa's backyard along with "the ballfield" where the little white fence adjacent to the near-by filling station was barely able to deflect his little brother's unbearable "foul tips" and from where grandpa would stand on the pitcher's mound and toss underhand in the shade of the apple tree's massive branches. And there was Old Joe, standing in the outfield, waiting for a chance to interrupt his daydream. Then, right when his lack of concentration was at its zenith, just like always, his little brother hit the ball to deep left-center field and into the high grass beneath the apple tree. So, once again, there went Old

Joe to search amongst the rotten apples and spider webs for the perfectly concealed baseball.

However, in an instant, the ballfield (along with the apple tree) was gone and had been replaced by mounds of dirt, and as Old Joe and his little brother stood there deciding upon how they should feel about this radical change they discovered the immense pleasure of throwing dirt clods into the air like hand grenades and watching them explode onto the barricades that guarded one another in their "new" field, which now resembled a combat zone in some foreign land. And for the next several hours, or what seemed like forever, they waged war on each other while never for an instant missing their old ballfield or the times they had shared upon it. Though, as dusk began to fall, Old Joe hurled one last "grenade" into the air and it crashed into his little brother's face. He ran away crying, with his hands covering his bloody nose and mouth.

But then, just as suddenly as before, the mounds of dirt were gone and Old Joe was back to being an old man who was now standing in the middle of a parking lot, where yellow lines intersected the blackness of the newly-laid asphalt.

And he found himself wanting to search amongst the rotten apples for his brother's long-lost baseball but, as he was standing alone in that vast piece of nothing, he was unable to recall where the apple tree had stood.

When he awoke, he wasn't quite sure what to make of this.

43.

It was a wondrous morning, with the clouds in the sky looking like freshly-pulled shreds of soft cotton candy and with another magnificent breeze blowing in gently from off the lake, as Old Joe went walking down Delaware and then made a bee line for the Chicken Patio.

Maybe it had something to do with the weather, or perhaps it was due to the tremendous amount of alcohol he'd consumed the night before, but normally he wouldn't be eating this early – though he might occasionally bum a handful of fries or maybe stop to grab a quick hot dog somewhere. However, after leaving the Beer Barrel with a couple of "Eddie B's" fantastic Bloody Marys under his belt, there had only been one thing on his mind – chicken.

Now the chicken at the Chicken Patio was always good, hence the name "Chicken Patio," but there were certain times when it was simply out of this world, or like Old Joe used to say, "Like you died and went to heaven."

And as it just so happened, this would be one of those times.

He was sitting there at a table and looking out at the lake, with his perfectly grilled breast of wine-basted barbecue chicken, along with a buttered roll and a corn on the cob and an ice-cold bottle of Coors Light, and while thoroughly enjoying all of the blessings of that incredible morning he began to realize once again just how fortunate he'd been to actually end up at Put-In-Bay.

"How many people," he thought, *"get a chance to live out their dreams?"*

So as he continued to look out at the lake, and at the clouds, and at that wonderful little downtown with its people all milling about, going to and fro, he took a nice-sized bite of his wonderful tasting chicken and then a long drink from his ice-cold bottle of Coors Light and thought, *"This is perfect."*

And that thought stayed with him.

44.

After he'd finished eating his lunch at the Chicken Patio, Old Joe remained sitting there and stared out at the lake, then he ordered a second beer and began thinking about another "perfect" day – one that had taken place a lifetime ago.

And though he sometimes had trouble remembering certain aspects of his young life, like learning to tie his shoes, or perhaps blowing out a few candles on his birthday cake, he could recall the events of this one day very well.

He was seven years old and playing in his family's front yard on a beautiful Saturday morning, with those billowing clouds and that crisp fresh air and with the crabapple tree ready to burst wide open. And he was bouncing a rubber ball off of the front stoop, and then sometimes the front door or over the roof, and then he went riding on his bicycle – down the driveway and back up again – and all the while his parents were busy with their spring cleaning.

And as his father was in the backyard washing the windows, he went inside and it smelled like lemons where his mother had been whirling around from room to room romantically dusting to the songs of Patti Page. However, his most vivid memory of that day was actually a single moment.

He was sitting on his bike at the bottom of the drive watching his parents, both at the same time, "framed" in happiness – his father through the breezeway in his white T-shirt and blue jeans with the backdrop of the world's greenest grass, while his mother at that very instant was captured singing in the kitchen window to one of her all-time favorite songs.

The classic tune to which she was listening was a most popular selection of the day titled the "Tennessee Waltz," a sweet yet haunting melody describing the angst of a lost love – along with its accompanying youthful innocence that can never be recaptured.

A moment in time – gone forever.

45.

Old Joe was sitting on his favorite barstool at the Beer Barrel.

He was more than halfway through his second of "Eddie B's" world famous Bloody Marys and had just ordered his third beer.

He'd brought his "journal" along with him just in case he found the energy to continue his project, "History Teacher – A Few of My Favorite Stories."

But it wasn't happening.

Instead, he was flipping through the pages and looking back at some of his older material, mostly some essays and short stories from over the years, when he came across a poem that he'd written about his mother, who had passed away almost twenty years earlier at the age of 76.

The poem was titled, "About You."

He took the sheet of paper that the poem was written on out of his three-ringed binder, held it up close to his failing eyes, and began to read:

About You

My mother gave me a poem to read,
that she'd found in the local obituaries,
titled, "A Mother's Farewell."
Instructions really, about how not to grieve
and not ever having to be alone,
even when that day comes for you,
that you would always be there
to welcome us home.
My mother, once again, thinking of others,
preparing well in advance
as is always the case,
very much before hand
to comfort us, even after she's gone.
But mother,
before there is such a poem written
about you, another one begins
and it goes something like this:
Some of the kindest words ever thought
or spoken, though not always heard,
so many times *from* you, about others.
But, my darling mother, who gives so much,
these beautiful thoughts are more times
about you, many times from others,
but so many more times
from me.

His mother never had the chance to read this poem; he'd been
in the process of writing it when she passed away unexpectedly.

143

And now, sitting there at the bar, Old Joe almost felt like crying.

But he didn't.

In fact, he couldn't remember the last time that he had.

46.

It was the third week of July and the day was hot – 89 by noon and climbing higher – and Old Joe was on his way to Frosty's from the Beer Barrel and he couldn't wait to get back into the shade.

When he walked into Frosty's it was "Johnny B. Goode" who immediately put a Coors Light down in front of him. "Oh, why thank you kemosabe," said Old Joe, "and may God always bless both you and your family." Then he picked up the bottle and on his initial attempt knocked it down about three-quarters of the way. "Ahh," he said, then he looked at Johnny and with a little smile he added, "I needed that."

Generally speaking, due to the prevailing westerly winds coming off of Lake Erie there weren't too many days during the summer which could be described as unpleasant; but, it was a good day to be out of the sun.

And that was just fine with Old Joe. After all, the old man's "game" was better suited these days for those fun indoor activities – like drinking.

However, even though he was still able to hold a decent conversation while sitting there and drinking his beer, his mind had been starting to wander off of late, and perhaps a little bit more than it should. There were times when his thoughts would be miles away, as if he were floating off somewhere in space, while still being seated right there at the bar.

Still knocking down a few cold ones.

Still talking his bullshit.

But on this day, he was staring at a "Buckeye Beer" advertisement that was hanging behind the bar. It was rectangular in shape with rounded edges and had a reflective surface in which the old man could see himself if he turned a certain way. And though it may have appeared that he was still sitting there at Frosty's, his mind had traveled backward in time to his old house in Toledo.

He was thinking about this one particular picture that used to hang on his basement wall, a drawing of a bald eagle, holding a banner in its beak with the words, "America Forever –1918." It was a fine example of primitive art with the eagle perched atop of Old Glory, and he remembered how its glass encasing used to capture his reflection whenever he would pass by.

As the story goes, Old Joe's grandfather used to own a downtown bar where this one hopeless drunk liked to hang out, and though the man was down on his luck and without the proverbial pot in which to piss he'd usually be given a free shot or two each day. And to paraphrase another old adage, *you should never buy a drunk a drink*; but Old Joe's grandfather had felt sorry for this man and was simply trying to ease his pain.

Then, one day, to his grandfather's complete surprise, the drunkard had shown up with this exceptional drawing of a bald eagle perched atop the American Flag to thank him for his kindness. And years later, when it was first presented to Old Joe, he'd instantly fallen in love with its artistry and considered it to be a burgeoning heirloom – having already been passed down through three generations and given lastly from his father to him.

Though now, after having gone through life with no children (or heirs) of his own, he was trying to recall just what he had done with that rather remarkable piece of artwork. He hadn't a clue.

And as he sat there, he noticed that "Johnny B. Goode" was still talking to him.

He'd been doing so all the while.

47.

For as hot as it had been those last few days it was a refreshingly cool morning, as Old Joe took his usual seat at the bar and put a hand in the air to say good-morning to "Eddie B."

"Hey Joe," said Eddie, "how are you on this fine morning?"

"Hangin' in there," he replied with a cough, "how you doin'?"

"Great – another day in paradise, right?"

"You know it kid," said Old Joe, "things could be a helluva lot worse."

"Very true," said Eddie, "very true."

"So, you want 'the big four?'"

"Um, yeah, sure – let's go for it."

"Ok boss, comin' right up."

Lately, Old Joe had been thinking a lot about the past and had gotten himself into a bit of a funk, but he was still bound and determined to continue his latest project so he'd once again brought along his "journal."

"Eddie B." brought over his water, then a Diet Coke along with a Coors Light, and he was in the process of making one of his amazing Bloody Marys when Old Joe opened his notebook and pulled out his pen.

He found where he had left off, with number "5" having been completed, then he looked over those last few paragraphs that he'd written about the Polish Cavalry in World War II. It read as follows:

So I guess it comes down to a single question that we all must answer, sooner or later: When the Grim Reaper knocks on your door and John Donne's bell begins to toll, would you rather go out charging on horseback against a Nazi tank – with a sword clenched in your bloody fist and screaming at the top of your lungs – or while sobbing into your pillow?

It's up to you.

Note: There've been a few reports in recent years debunking this story as a fable, as a wartime myth. However, some things in your heart you just know to be true.

Then he jotted down the number "6" and thought for a moment.

Then he wrote, "Jack Dempsey versus Jess Willard."

Now, having grown up in Toledo, Ohio, Old Joe was familiar with this story and had always been quite fond of the sport of boxing. In fact, when he was in his teens he'd actually competed in a few tournaments there in the old Westminster Gym.

So, after taking a quick swig of his beer, he began to write.

It was the world heavyweight championship fight.

July, 4, 1919, at Bay View Park in Toledo, Ohio.

In ungodly heat, well over one hundred degrees, with the sap from the make-shift split-rails oozing causing many of the gentlemen to lose their britches and then cover themselves with newspaper while wandering around the hastily-built eighty thousand seat stadium, the two fighters entered the ring. The famous western lawman Bat Masterson was collecting guns and knives at the gate, while trying to avoid any more shenanigans like the drunkards who had been caught bathing in the barrels of lemonade, thus ruining the lot for the folks who were getting hotter as the fight was ready to begin – and with Dempsey, "The Manassa Mauler," pouncing on the enormous Willard like a ferocious cat from the opening bell, and knocking him down seven times before being carried off by a frenzied and jubilant mob, only to have to return in the nick of time – under threat of disqualification – for the referee had never officially surrendered the match, to the chagrin of Dempsey's manager, who'd wagered most of his life's savings on a first round knock-out. However, the second and third rounds were just a formality for the beaten and battered Willard, and with his face now grotesquely disfigured – having been pummeled into relenting submission with five missing teeth and a broken jaw and several cracked ribs – the vanquished giant quietly boarded a train for home.

He stopped for a moment to take a sip from each one of his four drinks.

And though there was still much more to be written, of course, about the history of the two fighters and the incredible media coverage leading up to the match, it seemed that boxing had once more been the elixir that Old Joe needed.

He was feeling better.

48.

Old Joe was at Frosty's.

He was sitting at the bar and was mostly back to being his feisty self. He'd just seen a report of another terrorist attack on TV and wasn't in the mood to mince words.

"Fuck them," he said, "there's a special place in hell for those sons of bitches."

Then he heard someone to the right of him saying something about there being two sides to every story, and though Old Joe didn't make a habit out of butting in to other people's conversations, he immediately turned to the two men who were sitting there and asked, "What's that you said?" Both men looked to be somewhere in their thirties and the one sitting farthest away with curly dark hair said, "Why don't you mind your own business?"

Old Joe stood up from his barstool and said, "No, I'm not gonna mind my own business, because what I thought I heard you say was 'there's two sides to every story.' So if that's what you said, be man enough to repeat it."

Then the man with the curly dark hair turned and looked at Old Joe and said, "Sit down old man, before you get hurt."

A few weeks earlier, after having a few too many drinks and while sitting on the same barstool that he was now standing up from, Old Joe had mentioned something in a conversation with "Billy W." about trouble having a way of finding certain people – and how he believed that there were times in a man's life when he must be willing to fight. And at that time, Old Joe had said to Billy, "So if you happen to find yourself in a confrontation, one in which Jesus would turn the other cheek, here's what you should say:

'You know, I may be a lot of things, but the one thing that I'm not, is afraid of you.'" Then he said, "And when you say it, mean it! For the secret to winning that fight, or to winning any fight, is to not be afraid to lose – to take a punch, to throw a punch, to look like a fool, to bleed, or even, to one day die. Because then, no matter what happens, you've already won – as long as you remember to ask Jesus for forgiveness."

"Yeah, that's what I thought," said Old Joe, "look asshole, there aren't two sides to every story," then he pointed at the TV and said in a loud voice, "you see that right there – that's wrong! Plain and simple – so fuck you!"

Then the man stared straight back at Old Joe and said, "No, fuck you!"

And Old Joe retorted, "Hey, here's a thought – fuck you!"

Then the man got up from his barstool, but his friend put his hand on his shoulder and said, "Hey, he's not worth it – let's get the fuck outta here." Then both men got up and started for the door. But as he was leaving, the man with the curly dark hair turned back around and hoisted both of his middle fingers high in the air for everyone to see – especially Old Joe. And then, with a rather big smirk on his face, he and his friend walked over to the door and left. The old man watched them leave. Then he sat back down and drank his beer.

49.

"Fifteen down in the corner," said Old Joe.

It was his last ball on the table before the eight ball.

He was back at Frosty's playing a game of pool – a game of "eight-ball" to be more precise – with a kid that he'd just met from Findlay, Ohio.

They'd bet five bucks to make it "interesting."

Rather than roll for break, he gave the kid honors. His name was Andy and he seemed like a decent sort. But, when it came to anything competitive, that didn't matter – Old Joe was out to win.

After all, that's how he'd been raised, as a proud American capitalist who believed firmly in Adam Smith's "theory of self-interest." And being a former football player, Old Joe seemed to view each day as a newly-chalked gridiron with an ever-changing line of scrimmage, upon which he was always striving to gain yet another first down, and then another, and hoping to ultimately cross that fabled goal line – wherever it may be.

Though, sometimes, he simply enjoyed a well-played game of pool.

The kid had a nice break and pocketed two balls, both solids, before missing.

Then Old Joe missed his first shot, when he attempted to bank the nine-ball into the middle pocket on a crowded table.

Then Andy went a bit ape-shit – and made four in a row – before missing a wide open two-ball in the corner pocket which almost certainly would've given him the game, since the eight-ball looked to be a "bunny" resting just a few inches from that same pocket.

So, when Old Joe walked back up to the table, he had some work to do. Andy had one ball left on the table while he had seven – and then, of course, the eight-ball.

Old Joe loved this game. There had been a pool table in the basement of his parents' house when he was growing up, and he had played hundreds of games, if not thousands. He loved the geometry of the game, the angles, the precision – he even loved the colors of the balls, the solids and the stripes, and the sounds they made as they went crashing into one another.

He would begin his comeback by attempting the nine-ball again, that beautiful ball with the yellow stripe and cool-looking number "9." And if he made it, the table would "open-up" because he could see how every other shot was going to line-up perfectly in a beautifully arranged sequential pattern. That is, if he could make this delicate little cut-shot first, where he had to barely nip the ball or "cut-it" into the side pocket.

Old Joe got low into his stance. That was his secret, what had always made him such a good player, his bending of the knees to where his line of sight was almost directly at table level. To him, it was like staring through the scope of a rifle. And then, with a very fluid motion and thrusting of his cue stick, that nice white cue ball would go exactly where he was aiming – unless, of course, he was totally hammered.

However, that wasn't the case this afternoon.

He made the shot.

Now the table was his – and he knew it.

He made his next five shots in a row, which were all relatively easy, four in the corner and one in the side, and now all that was standing between him and the game was the fifteen-ball – that pretty little baby with the dark brown stripe and that bold number "15" printed in black – which he made as well.

Only the eight-ball remained.

It was sitting right next to the corner pocket, only inches away. However, over the centuries, many a game has been lost by scratching on the eight-ball.

Though, being the veteran player that he was, Old Joe could've simply put back-spin on the cue ball to stop it dead in its tracks after striking the eight-ball and sending it home. But, then again, in order to do this he would have to strike the cue ball low and with some force, and since he was using a slightly bowed stick with a rounded tip, he decided against it.

Instead, he calmly called "eight-ball corner pocket."

And then he sent the cue ball on its way – slowly, slowly, to gently kiss the eight-ball into the corner pocket and come neatly to rest. That was it.

Game over.

50.

It was already 82 degrees at a quarter 'til 10 on another steamy July day, as Old Joe entered the Beer Barrel.

"Top of the mornin' to ya," said Eddie.

"And the rest of the day to you my lad," replied Old Joe.

It was becoming quite obvious that these two men enjoyed their daily ritual.

"What's that you got there? Oh no, not another book from Sarita."

"Very funny," said Old Joe, as he plopped himself down in a barstool. "No kid, this is something called poetry, I picked it up at the library – you know, that one building over there where they actually serve up a little culture and don't give their customers such a hard time."

"Poetry?" continued Eddie. "You can't be serious."

"Oh, come on now," said Old Joe, "it's not that bad."

"Not that bad?" repeated the young bartender as he went about making Old Joe's Bloody Mary, "Ya' know Joe, I'm beginning to have my doubts about you."

Old Joe smiled. He loved to joke around with "Eddie B."

But, in actual fact, he had always liked poetry – and he'd even tried his hand at writing a few verses. To him, each poem was a little story unto itself. So lately, instead of a novel, where he would always find himself going back to remember what he'd previously read and then looking to see where he'd left off, he'd been spending more of his time reading a poem or two and then simply enjoying the dozen or so lines that he'd just finished.

For Old Joe, it was a good fit.

And as he sat back in his barstool with his Coors Light and Bloody Mary, there was one poem in particular that had caught his eye.

It was titled, *"Across the Street from the Funeral Home,"* and it reminded him of that dream he'd had a week or so earlier – the one he'd had so much trouble understanding – where he'd been left standing in the middle of an empty parking lot in what had once been his grandpa's backyard. The poem read as follows:

Yellow lines crisscross the blacktop
where children like to play
where the foul balls and home runs
are cursed and chased
as they continue to roll like marbles
on the sidewalk
against their young pursuers' wishes

and in spite of their thrown mitts
and where there is recent moisture
from sweat and spit
whenever cars are not parked there
for special occasion.

When he was done, Old Joe turned the book over and with its pages spread open placed it down gently upon the bar. Then he leaned back in his barstool and took a good long drink from his Bloody Mary.

He was thinking about the poem.

"*The years roll by,*" he thought, "'*like marbles on the sidewalk,*' *and you can't stop 'em, no matter what you do. Not the bad ones or the good ones – the 'foul balls and home runs' – not by 'cursing,' or even by throwing a baseball mitt.*"

Then he picked up the book and looked again.

"*And so that empty lot across the street,*" he continued, "*that's for extra parking – to be used only on 'special occasion.' Like when some-one dies. Maybe someone important? Someone with a lot of friends.*"

His dream was beginning to make sense.

51.

It was three in the afternoon when like clockwork Old Joe entered The Roundhouse.

He hadn't been there for more than a minute when Sherri came up to him and asked, "Where were you yesterday?"

"Oh," he replied grudgingly, "I went back to my room to take a nap and over-slept."

"Another nap? I don't know Old Joe, it sounds to me like you might be losin' your edge a little bit."

"Not likely," he said, "that's one thing you'll never have to worry about with me."

Old Joe liked "Sherri darlin." He liked her very much, especially her honesty – and sometimes, her bluntness. She was from a small town in Indiana called Goshen, about twenty miles southwest of Shipshewana, and he appreciated the fact that she was straight-forward with no hidden agendas. He'd once heard her say to some ass-hole customer, "Hey, don't piss down my back and tell me it's rainin'!" Old Joe just loved that – it was something his grandpa used to say.

He actually preferred those people who were a little rough around the edges, the ones who would say it like it is, and tell you where you stand – even if they didn't like you but would at least tell you that to your face – rather than someone who was only pretending to be a friend.

Then Sherri used her old line, "So, when we goin' out?" and Old Joe (thinking that this time he'd mess around with her a little) replied, "Ya' know, you keep saying that, but if I ever took you up on your offer it would probably scare the hell out of ya.'" But, once again, without missing a beat she retorted, "If you ever took me up on my offer I think that we'd have one helluva good time. We could do shots all night long – whaddaya say?" "Oh boy," he said, "I'll tell ya' what kid – that might be a tad much for me these days," and as she was walking away to wait on her next table she replied, "Well, you'll never know 'til you try."

The band was on break, so he could hear himself think for once, and the place had recently been hosed down so all of that wet wood smelled terrific – and he'd actually been able to find a seat along the west side's rounded and elongated wall. So he was sitting there opposite the restrooms and waiting for the singers to come back on stage when "little Becky" came charging up like she always did, as if she were riding on the back of a motor scooter. Then she abruptly stopped and said, "Hey stranger, where were you yesterday? You had us worried."

Then Old Joe said, "You know, I've already been through all of this with your twin sister over there – you guys should start carrying around some walkie-talkies or somethin." "Walkie-talkies?" she asked, "what are those? Oh, are those the things that they used to use in the Army? We have cell phones nowadays Old Joe, so why would we do that?" The girl talked a mile a minute and then, as always, she would stand there and stare straight into his eyes until receiving an answer that she deemed to be acceptable. So, this time, Old Joe simply said, "Becky, sweetheart, you know I love ya', but you should probably get back to work."

"Ok," she said, rather matter-of-factly, then added, "I love you too Old Joe," before taking off like a rocket again.

Then he watched her as she began waiting on tables and he started laughing to himself. As with Sherri, he simply thought the world of "little Becky." But how could he not? She was perhaps even more straight-forward than Sherri, if that were possible, in the way that she would look at people and talk to them, and even in the way she would come up to them, *"like a bat outta hell,"* he thought. And though they weren't actually twin sisters, or sisters at all, one might've assumed such a thing since they looked alike – both cute little blondes with those twenty-something bodies – and since Becky had been trained for this job by Sherri and had taken on many of her characteristics.

But now he needed a beer and thought, *"Where'd they go?"*

And then the band began to play.

52.

Later that same evening, after stopping by to see both Sarita and Diago for only a beer or two, Old Joe went back to his motel room. He was tired and fell asleep quickly and had yet another dream.

It was night-time and he was older, though not yet an old man, and he'd returned to the neighborhood in which he had lived as a child. And though unsure at first, as he kept walking along he could feel each step becoming more comfortable, like a pair of fading blue jeans. He recognized the working-class porches and shutters, with their weariness imperceptible through the darkness, having been masked with earthy emeralds and auburns, thus appearing quite deep and rich while reflecting the glancing blows of light being thrown by a punch-drunk moon, now giddy with sentiment and disobeying the night by having reunited their shadows. And with each additional step, his ease grew, like a stack of Sunday-morning flapjacks, as that familiar smell of the trees washed over him like syrup. However, as he continued along, he suddenly realized that he was late for school and by the time he arrived the bell had already rung. And the old playground, though somewhat reminiscent, more resembled some foreign land once visited, with eerie wrought-iron gates and name-less markers for the dead. But he enjoyed the fact that he could still dissect the maze, that he could navigate its passage evenly and with-out effort, though the child-sized stairs now seemed unnatural, and barely negotiable, when taken one at a time.

For the most part, it was a peaceful night's sleep.

53.

After spending the morning talking to Eddie and writing a few more thoughts down in his "journal," Old Joe left the Beer Barrel and returned to his motel room to drop off that rather cumbersome three-ring binder. Then he decided to go for a walk through Perry Park and take his "indirect route" to Frosty's. So he headed north up Catawba, retracing his steps, until crossing at Delaware Avenue.

It was already quarter past noon and the sidewalks and streets were beginning to fill up with people, with still more of those happy, excited, pretty young faces coming off of the Jet Express. But as he stood near the corner of Catawba and Bayview Old Joe could hear the hubbub growing louder, so he suddenly changed his mind about going for a walk through the park and went left toward the Put-In-Bay Winery instead.

Where last evening he could only hear the sounds of the waves as they were gently lapping against the tied-off boats and schooners, he now continued to walk a little farther down the bay trying to distance himself from the crowd.

But after his nerves began to settle and as he was moseying along peeking inside some of the gift shop windows, he abruptly changed course and walked straight toward a big hill with its alluring patterns of freshly-mown grass. Then he eventually found himself going down a series of small steps and through a red-bricked alleyway aligned with flower boxes and hanging baskets, and after going to wherever the wind might take him he ended up at a place that he'd never been – the Lake Erie Island Historical Museum. There was a nominal admission fee for seniors of four dollars, so Old Joe handed the lady behind the counter a ten and said, "Here you go darlin', keep the change."

And as it turned out, being that he was still just an old-fashioned history teacher at heart, this place was an absolute feast for his eyes – with more documents and photographs than he could shake a stick at and with a treasure-trove of Native American artifacts. There were bows, arrows, knives, war clubs, spears, tomahawks, spear-throwers, head-dresses, dream-catchers and lances – not to mention a plethora of arrowheads. And all of these objects had originated from the various Lake Erie tribes: The Miami, Iroquois, Shawnee, Chippewa, Delaware, Erie, Ottawa, Kickapoo, Huron, Kaskaskia, and Potawatomi.

Then, of course, with the actual fighting having taken place off the coastline of this very island, there was also the complete history of the ever-popular "Battle of Lake Erie." It might be difficult for some visitors to grasp at first but, even though the exploits of Commodore Perry are known around the world, there is no place on earth where this man is more celebrated than here at Put-In-Bay. In other words, Commodore Oliver Hazard Perry and South Bass

Island have become almost synonymous – pretty much, one and the same.

Old Joe was like a kid in a candy store.

Though when he was finished, and had seemingly gotten his fill, he went around back and made yet another discovery. There was a dirt path leading to an old red barn (that had clearly seen its better days) with a sign above the door reading "The Re-Sale Shop" and when he walked inside and took his first look around he became amazed all over again.

The list of items he saw included the following: books, lamps, desks, dressers, hats, clothes, jewelry, hammers, saws, screwdrivers, paints, pens, pencils, crayons, stuffed animals, mannequins and much, much more. He may've even found a heffalump and a woozle if he had searched long enough, but thought it might be best at that point to move along. (Though he was quite certain that he'd only seen the tip of the iceberg!)

So with these new wonders of the island still swimming around in his head he exited out the back door and continued on with his journey. He was now heading southward and came upon a long hedge-line that was running from east to west, and after finding a small opening and taking a step inside it was as if he had somehow entered a different world.

There was an enormous lawn, beautifully manicured, resembling an old-style English croquet field, and then another massive yard that was hidden behind some more hedges, and then another one beyond even that.

And all of these estates had wonderful gardens, with all sorts of plants and flowers and whirligigs, and one even reminded him of the Palace of Versailles with its canopies and fountains and statues.

But by this time, Old Joe had stopped walking.

He was just standing now, occasionally turning and then looking all around. He remained in that last garden for quite some time. He probably could've stayed for an eternity.

It was one of the most divine places that he'd ever seen.

No one knew he was there.

54.

Old Joe was running behind schedule. He'd overslept.

So it was already past nine in the evening when he entered The Boathouse and took his now customary seat on a wooden bench alongside the front wall.

He was tired. So even before he scanned the place for Sarita he closed his eyes for a few minutes and sat there.

Then, when he opened them, she was standing right in front of him. She had a way of doing that, showing up when he wasn't expecting her to be there.

"What's wrong Papa," she asked, "are you sleepy again?"

"Yes honey," he answered, "I'm a little tired."

"You're not getting enough rest – that's not good for you."

"Yeah, I know," he said, "but I'll do some catching up tonight."

"I brought you a beer – do you still want it?"

"Oh sure, I'll take it." Then he reached into his pocket and pulled out a twenty and said, "Here you go sweetie, thanks."

Then Sarita said, "Thank you Papa, now close your eyes and get some rest and I'll be back to check on you, ok?"

"All right honey," he replied, "but I'll be fine."

Then before turning to walk away she said, "Take care of yourself Joe."

He smiled and said, "You know it kid."

And then, after watching her disappear into the crowd, he sat there holding his beer and began looking at the label which read, "BORN IN THE ROCKIES, EST'D 1978," and the mountains were blue.

However, without taking a drink, he sat the bottle down next to him on the bench.

And then he left.

55.

Though trying his best to muddle through, Old Joe was in a funk again.

His mind had been wandering more than usual.

And he wasn't sure if these two things were somehow related – or if the cause and the effect were the same.

Maybe he wasn't focusing enough on the present because he'd been concerning himself too much with the past, or perhaps it was the simple fact that he was getting old. Or it could've been a lack of sleep, or his cancer, or a dozen other things – but he just didn't feel right.

Something was amiss.

And though he couldn't quite put his finger on it, he wasn't himself.

So after leaving The Boathouse, along with his full bottle of Coors Light, he crossed Hartford Avenue and went walking through Perry Park. He stopped for a moment underneath the large trees to listen to the gentle rustling of the leaves, then continued along while looking around at all of the neon lights on Delaware and Catawba, from The Roundhouse all the way down to Mojito Bay.

He took a long look across the way at the Chicken Patio, and then a little farther down the line to Frosty's and then to the Beer Barrel. *"How beautiful,"* he thought, *"all of those different colors."*

Old Joe loved colors. Ever since he was a child he had loved everything about them.

He loved their names.

Red. Yellow. Blue.

So simple. So perfect.

He loved seeing their names on the side of a crayon.

Orange. Green. Purple.

He loved seeing them arranged in a brand new box of 64 and how they complimented one another.

He loved seeing them in gardens, and on billiard balls as they went rolling across a felt-covered table. And, perhaps especially, he loved how vibrant they remained after coming to rest. When random. When in a state of happenstance.

Then his mind began to wander back to an early morning in his family's basement, after his father and his buddies had quit playing pool but with the smoke from their cigars still hanging in the room. He remembered how as a child he'd snuck down the steps around two in the morning just to sit there by himself and look at all of those exquisitely scattered billiard balls that were still lying upon the table.

He loved those colors. He loved that smell.

And as he sat on those downstairs steps, next to the bar and pool table, he realized how each ball was simply a varying degree of the others, like the color wheel at his school.

And he thought, *"How perfect."*

He loved how life was like an unfinished game.

56.

Old Joe was dying.

His cancer had spread.

He'd known this for some time. In fact, that's why he'd come back to Put-In-Bay, because he knew that this would be his last summer – and he had planned to spend all of his money by Labor Day.

However, he'd been feeling out of sorts of late – and didn't know why.

But then, he sat up in bed.

It was 4 o'clock in the morning and he had just had an idea.

He'd had a great idea.

"It doesn't have to be Labor Day," he thought, *"I can choose to die whenever I want."*

And instantly, he began to feel better.

Then he made a new plan.

He decided to forget about his whole Labor Day idea and to give away the rest of his money – and like a bolt of lightning from out of the blue he was suddenly full of energy.

He hadn't felt this excited in a very long time.

The only questions now were "to whom to give the money?" and "how much?" So he jumped out of bed and got his old gym bag down from the ceiling.

And then, stack by stack, he began to count.

57.

He'd been trying all summer to spend his money. Only now, Old Joe wished that there was more.

What remained inside of that old gym bag, which would've been fine just a few days earlier – and easily taken him to his original goal of Labor Day if not beyond – was to say the least, disappointing.

A total of $32,500.00.

"Why didn't I think of this sooner?" he thought.

And then, once again, he began to wonder, *"Who should I give it to?"*

Then his very next thought was, *"And how much?"*

The first two people who came to mind, of course, were Diago and Sarita.

Diago was like a son to him. And Sarita may've been the love that he'd been searching for his entire life.

However, he also knew that "Eddie B." could use some money.

Along with "Big Sal" and "Billy W." and "Johnny B. Goode."

In fact, there were quite a few people on the island who could've used some help. So, as Old Joe thought more about this, he started to become more upset. *"I shouldn't have blown my money like that,"* he thought, *"and done this sooner."* He'd always been a generous tipper, throwing mostly twenties around and some times more – but to him, this was different. This wasn't a gratuity or an act of required reciprocity, rather it was his attempt (no matter how late in the game) to show these good people some actual kindness.

Though now, he was sorry that he couldn't do more.

And that was one of the reasons why it was so difficult for him to decide to whom to give the money, because there simply wasn't enough of it to go around. He wished that he could somehow reach into his old gym bag and pull out a million dollars for each of them – but, he was going to have to work with what he had.

So, eventually, he made a list of the eight people he knew the best and cared for the most:

Diago
Sarita
Eddie
Sal
Bill
John
Sherri
Becky

"And now," he thought, *"all I have to do is put the dollar amounts next to their names."*

But, once more, therein was the rub.

58.

For the rest of that day, Old Joe laid low.

He mostly stayed in his room drinking beer and thinking.

Every now and then, with the shades drawn, he would sit there and recount the money. However, he did go to the carry-out to pick up some more beer and to buy a sleeve of those little brown bags that people use when packing their lunches. He needed something bigger than the letter envelopes he had and thought that these bags would make for a nicer "package" when delivering the money.

He also purchased a black magic marker and some masking tape.

Then, back in his motel room, he began printing the names of the eight people on the list – as neatly as he could – onto the bags. And he used their nicknames, the ones he'd always called them; "Eddie B.," "Big Sal," "Billy W.," "Johnny B. Goode," "Sherri darlin'," "little Becky," and of course, "Diago" and "Sarita."

"Oh Sarita," he thought.

"How will I be able to do this?"

And he still hadn't decided exactly how much money he was going to give to each person.

This was going to require a twelve-pack of Coors Light, at the very least, and some serious thinking. He opened up his first beer and went to work.

At first, he thought about splitting the money up evenly, with that being the "fair" thing to do. But then he thought, *"Fuck it – it's my money. I'll be the one to decide what's fair."*

And when he was being truly honest with himself, it always came back to the two people on this planet that he loved the most – Diago and Sarita.

So, eventually, he decided that both of them would receive the "lion's share" while the rest of the money would be divided equally amongst the others. And then, once again, he began to feel somewhat sheepish that there wasn't more.

However, since nothing could be done about that at this point, he decided to refocus his attention back upon the brown paper bags.

The money was in stacks of twenties, with a thousand dollars per stack.

He gave both Diago and Sarita ten stacks, or ten thousand dollars, while everyone else received two. And, each time, Old Joe would make sure to double-bag. He would put the money into one of the little brown paper bags, fold it up, and then put that bag inside of the one with the person's name already neatly printed on the outside. Then he folded that bag as well and made sure that it was securely taped. When he was done, he put all eight of the "packages" into his old gray gym bag, grabbed another beer, and tried to find a game on TV.

And then, a few hours later, he stored the bag away and went to bed.

He slept like a baby.

59.

Old Joe awakened that next morning feeling better than he had in years. So he quickly went through his routine then grabbed his old gym bag and with a smile on his face headed out the door.

It was the first day of August, still a month or so before Labor Day, and you could feel the heat rising from the street as Old Joe took his familiar path down Catawba and then turned right onto Delaware Avenue.

His first stop, per usual, was the Beer Barrel. He wanted to see "Eddie B." to drop-off his cash, of course, but he also had a monstrous craving for one of his stupendous Bloody Marys. However, his intention was to stay somewhat clear-headed, because he knew that he had a very long day ahead of him that was certain to become even longer if he didn't. And it wasn't so much that he was worried about an entire day of drinking, for that had never concerned him in the past, but he was now toting around a bag which contained some thirty-two thousand dollars, so the last thing he wanted was to get sloppy.

"Hey there chief – how ya' doin' this mornin'?" said Eddie.

"Just fine kid, how 'bout yourself?"

"Oh, you know, still livin' the dream – I just cleaned up some puke in the bathroom."

"No shit?" said Old Joe, then he added, "pardon the pun," which put a smile on Eddie's face.

"That's a good one Joe – say, are you available for any kids parties?"

"Anytime," he said, "just let me know."

Then Eddie put a cold bottle of Coors Light down in front of him and said, "Hey man, it's good to see you smile."

"Thanks buddy," said the old man, and then he took a swig of his beer as he looked out at the distant water of Lake Erie. It was a quarter 'til ten and even though the temperature was already hovering somewhere around eighty it felt magnificent sitting there in the shade. There was a slight breeze coming in from off the lake as the old man took another drink of his beer, and then in a soft voice he said, "Thank you Lord for letting me see this day." Eddie came back with a water and a Diet Coke, then he returned a minute or so later with a Bloody Mary.

"You good Joe?" asked Eddie. "You need anything else?"

Old Joe looked Eddie right in the eyes and said, "Never been better."

"Ok buddy, holler if you need anything."

Then, for the next few hours, the old man just sat there taking in the sights and feeling that incredible breeze. Though, whenever

Eddie would pass by, the two of them would shoot the shit for a while.

But it was going on noon and the place was starting to get a little crowded so Old Joe began looking more and more at that old gym bag sitting in the barstool next to his. "This is going to be a little harder than I thought," said Old Joe, once again quietly and to himself, "just how in the hell am I going to do this exactly?" Then he started thinking about Eddie, and knowing him like he did, he figured that he might not want to accept a gift of money and be seen as some sort of charity case. After all, "Eddie B." was the quintessential "hard worker" who'd earned everything that he ever had. Quite simply, it's who the man was. However, Old Joe also knew that Eddie was an incredibly nice guy, a great human being, who would do anything he could to help anyone. So he thought the best way to approach this would be to ask Eddie for a favor because – being the kind person that he was – he wouldn't refuse.

Furthermore, while running different scenarios through his mind, Old Joe thought that it might be a better idea to give "Big Sal's" package to Eddie as well – so that he could give it to him when the two men saw each other later in the day. Originally, Old Joe had thought that it would be best to hand deliver all of the "packages" because, let's face it, it was a lot of money. But, as he sat there thinking for a moment, a smile came to his face and he thought, *"If you can't trust a person like 'Eddie B.,' then who in the hell can you trust?"* Besides, this would save him a trip back to the Beer Barrel and from having to go through this whole awkward process again. *"And Sal can be a bit touchy about certain things,"* he thought, *"so I wouldn't want to embarrass the big fella."*

And that's when he decided just what it was that he was going to do.

He put a few bills down on the counter to cover his tab and motioned for Eddie to come over. The young bartender held up a finger as if to say, *"Hold on just a minute,"* then he walked over and said, "Hey Joe, whaddaya need?" And Old Joe replied, "Um, I've got somethin' here for ya' – but I need you to do me a favor."

And Eddie said, "You got somethin' – what is it?" Then Old Joe reached into his old gym bag and pulled out the brown paper sack with "Eddie B." printed on the outside, and then while handing it to Eddie he said, "Well, that's the favor you see – I can't tell you what it is – and I need you to promise that you won't open it until tomorrow."

"Seriously?" said Eddie.

"Yeah, but that's not all. I also need you to give this one to Sal with the same caveat – he can't open it until tomorrow." Then Old Joe pulled out the brown paper sack with "Big Sal" printed on it and handed that "package" to Eddie as well.

Then he looked at him and asked, "Are we good?"

And after pausing for a moment, Eddie replied, "Um, well, you got me guessing here a little bit Old Joe – I mean, I know it's not drugs or anything, right?"

And the old man shook his head and said, "No, of course not."

Then Eddie said, "Well, ok then, if that's what you want."

"All right," said Old Joe, "you're sure now?"

"Yeah," replied Eddie, "I'm sure – you have my word."

"Well, that's good enough for me," said the old man.

Then he stood up and shook Eddie's hand.

"See ya' partner," he said.

"Ok Joe, take care," said Eddie, "I'll see you tomorrow."

"You bet," replied Old Joe. Then he picked up his old gym bag and walked away.

He left a twenty dollar tip.

60.

One of the more fortunate things about Old Joe's plans for the day was that they didn't deviate from his normal routine. Thus, on paper, it all looked fairly simple – since the people to whom he wanted to give the "packages" were not only going to be working at the establishments he was visiting but they would also be there at the same times.

After all, that's how he'd become acquainted with each of them in the first place – and discovered what truly good people all of them were.

And, for the most part, he was pretty satisfied with the way things had started out at the Beer Barrel with "Eddie B." and (although indirectly) "Big Sal," so while taking the short walk eastward on Delaware Avenue he was hoping to have the same kind of luck with both "Billy W." and "Johnny B. Goode" at Frosty's.

Now, you may have noticed that Old Joe liked to use nicknames – and that he used them whenever possible.

However, the old man didn't do this simply because he thought that they were fun and cool, which they most certainly were, but also because they seemed to help his failing memory – especially when he got drunk (which he almost always was) – by attaching a name to a face.

But, unlike "Eddie B." and "Big Sal," who were known by their nicknames to practically everyone on the island, when it came to both "Billy W." and "Johnny B. Goode," Old Joe was the person who'd come up with these names; therefore, he was the only one who would address the young men in this manner. And like Old Joe, "Billy W." (who also went by Bill, Billy, or sometimes even "Billy the Kid") was of Polish descent and had one of those last names that no one could pronounce. So, right off the bat, Old Joe had felt a connection with the big red-headed kid along with a certain amount of empathy. And as for the moniker "Johnny B. Goode," well, that one was always considered to have been a "lay-up" for Old Joe – and had obviously come from the old Chuck Berry song.

And as he came through the door it seemed like your typical day, with his favorite barstool near the back hallway still available, even though both the bar and restaurant sections were mostly filled. Old Joe said "hey" to "Johnny B. Goode" but didn't see Bill right off the bat, which had him worried for a second or two, but then John told him that the big red head was working the back patio, so Old Joe settled in and ordered his beer.

Then John put a Coors Light down in front of the old man and asked, "So whatcha been up to old-timer – stayin' out of prison?"

"Barely," he replied, "and how 'bout you? Everything ok?"

"Oh, pretty good Old Joe, thanks for askin.'"

Then "Johnny B. Goode" walked away. And usually, that was the extent of it between these two. At least, until Old Joe got a little drunk, then he'd like to bend John's ear on all sorts of things, including his philosophies on life and his advice for the world – which were at times priceless. But today, Old Joe wasn't planning on getting too shit-faced, so after he finished his beer he got up from his barstool and walked through the hallway to the back patio.

By this time the temperature had reached the mid 80's, but if you were lucky enough to get a seat at the Tiki bar there was usually a nice breeze coming through the alleyway that led out to one of the large hotels.

And, once again, someone from above must've been smiling on Old Joe because the best seat in the house had just opened up. It was the corner barstool nearest the alley, and you really couldn't get much better than that. So with that little thatch roof providing some shade and a freshly iced-down trough of cold Coors Light, Old Joe could definitely see himself sitting there for a while and shooting the shit with "Billy W."

Bill walked over and said, "How ya' doin' Joe, can I get you a Coors Light?" "Most definitely my good man, most definitely – so I see they got you workin' in the sticks." Bill smiled and said, "Yeah, what's a guy to do? It's like they always say Old Joe, I'd complain – but who'd listen?"

"Oh, don't I know it kid – don't I know it."

"Say, how's that little girlfriend of yours doin'? What's her name again?"

"Danielle."

"Yeah, that's right, Danielle. You'd better watch it there boy – she's a real good-looker."

"Yeah, I know – I think I may've out-punted my coverage a little on this one."

"Oh boy, you're tellin' me," said Old Joe. "You're damned right you did! Just try not to screw it up."

"I'll do my best," said Billy.

Then they continued their conversation intermittently, with Billy having to excuse himself every now and then to go wait on the other customers, while Old Joe sat there just as content as he could be – with a nice breeze, a comfortable barstool, a little thatch roof, and an ice cold beer.

So for the next hour or two he kept sitting there, drinking his beer and enjoying the scenery, only getting up a few times to go to the john. Other than that, he was thinking about how to deliver his little brown paper packages in the best manner possible.

But, once again, he was a bit stymied, because what had worked with "Eddie B." probably wouldn't work here.

"I can't just give them both a brown package and say 'wait 'til tomorrow,' he thought, *"because you know damn well that 'Johnny B. Goode' won't wait – he'll open it, sure as shit – and then, once he found out that it was money that was in there, what would he think? No, I can't take that chance,"* thought the old man, *"I'm gonna have to come up with something else."*

Old Joe had put himself on the spot and he was going to have to do some fast thinking.

He thought, *"In 'Eddie B.'s' case, I relied on his good-heartedness and honesty, but in this situation I'm gonna have to lie."* And it wasn't that he didn't trust the boys so much, either "Billy W." or "Johnny B. Goode" for that matter, it's just that this was sort of an odd thing and he needed an idea that would cover all the bases.

But then, right when he needed it most, Old Joe had a moment of brilliance. *"Scratch-offs,"* he thought, *"that'll work."*

And the old man began to smile.

You see, for all of his life Old Joe had seen himself as a problem solver, and he believed that this matter in particular had deserved a little mulling over.

Because, even though most people wouldn't walk past a quarter that was lying on the sidewalk, the situation becomes a little different when the money (no matter how small the amount) is actually presented to those same people as a gift – and even more so if it comes out of left field – because then the obvious response is to ask the question "why?" And that's what Old Joe was trying his very best to avoid.

And even if the old man's answer to that question was something like, "Well, this is for all of the times that I should've tipped you a little more this summer," the question would then become, "why now?" And that wasn't much better. He needed to give both boys a plausible explanation – one that was good enough to have them not only accept the money, but to also have them *not* ask "why?" And the issue was further complicated by the fact that he didn't want to make the young men feel guilty in any way. These were the kinds of things that Old Joe was thinking about.

After all, that's who he was – a thinker.

He was a prodigious thinker.

He would think about all sorts of things all of the time and then run different scenarios through his mind – like he had in this instance – before coming up with the right idea.

"Scratch-offs!"

Brilliant.

Especially for such a "black and white" guy like himself. A man who believed that things were either right or wrong and didn't much care for any "gray area." Yes, this would work.

And Old Joe was feeling pretty damn proud of himself.

Because, the way he had it figured, all he would have to say was that he came into some extra money via this "lottery ticket" and he wanted both men to share in his good fortune. Simple.

Even nice guys such as these wouldn't have a problem accepting money with an explanation like that – right? And there would be no need for either suspicion or guilt. Perfect.

So he motioned for "Billy W." to come over and then leaned over the bar as he was approaching and said in a soft voice, "Hey, um, Billy, I got a little somethin' here for ya." Then he reached into his old gym bag and pulled out the brown paper bag with "Billy W." printed on it and said, "I had some luck on one of those 'scratch-off' tickets the other day and I wanted to share a little bit of the good fortune with you – so here ya' go." But as he began to give him the package "Billy W." said, "What – money? No, I couldn't take any of your winnings from you like that Old Joe, that's yours. But thanks for thinking of me."

"No, seriously kid, I want you to have it – here."

"Thanks Joe, but no, really, you keep that – ok?"

"Oh for Christ's sake Bill," he replied, "what the fuck's your problem – make an old man happy, would ya'?"

"Well, if you really want me to have it."

"Just take the damned thing!"

"Billy W." hesitated for another moment but finally accepted the package and said, "Ok, thanks a lot Joe." And the old man replied, "Don't mention it."

Then he grabbed his gym bag and said, "All right kid, I gotta go, I'll see ya' around," and just like that he left with "Billy W." shouting behind him, "Ok, thanks again. I'll see you tomorrow."

Old Joe walked back through the hallway and re-entered Frosty's main bar. He hurried down toward the far end where "Johnny B. Goode" was standing and in a half-raised voice said, "Hey Johnny, come here a minute." Thus, obligingly, the young barkeep strolled over and after they had both leaned in a little ways toward each other he said, "Yeah Joe, what's up?" Then, in almost a whisper, the old fella said, "Hey, uh, I was just talkin' with your 'partner in crime' back there and told him that I had a little luck the other day on one of those 'scratch-off' tickets and uh, as I was tellin' Bill, I want to share it with you guys, so here." But, once again, as he went to give him the package "Johnny B. Goode" said, "What – money?"

"Jesus Christ," thought Old Joe, *"here we go again."*

"Oh, thanks Joe but – no, I can't take your money like that."

"Look, it's for all the shit I put you through, ok?"

"No buddy, really, I can't."

Then Old Joe shouted, "Johnny, would you just shut the fuck up and take the money."

"Well, geez Joe, you don't have to get all violent and everything."

"Take it!"

"Ok, ok." Then "Johnny B. Goode" reached out and took the little brown package with his name printed on it and said, "Thanks Joe, this is really nice."

"Sure kid," said the old man, "no problem."

Then, as Old Joe started walking toward the door, he put his left hand in the air to indicate "good-bye" and said, "All right, take care."

And "Johnny B. Goode" shouted after him, "Ok, you too, see ya' tomorrow."

But he was already gone.

He'd done it.

He'd actually walked out of Frosty's – the place where it all began.

Then he turned right and started walking eastward down Delaware Avenue toward The Roundhouse.

And as he started thinking about how things had just transpired with "Billy W." and "Johnny B. Goode," a little smile came to his face and in a calm and measured voice he said, "Piece of cake."

61.

As Old Joe approached The Roundhouse, he thought about all of the times that he'd been there before and how he'd come to love that old, red building as if it were a member of his own family.

When he went inside it felt like home, with the muted sunlight and those dark hardwood floors, and with that oversized tapestry hanging from the ceiling in those patriotic colors of red, white and blue.

And with the music playing and the people laughing, and with that scent of freshness mixed with beer, he remembered back to that time when he'd first been here, when he thought, *"There's no place quite like this."* And after all these years and all those bars later, he was now more convinced of that first impression than ever before, as "Sherri darlin'" walked up and shouted over the music, "Hey old man, when we goin' out?" To which he replied, "Oh, I don't know, you look like some trouble to me," and she gave him a smile and said, "I'll go grab you a beer," then as she was making her way back through that big crowd Old Joe looked around and thought, *"Wow, it's good to have friends."* And though the place was packed with "standing room only," Old Joe didn't mind in the least, he was just happy to be enjoying the festivities and to be out among the living. And as he was watching the people around him "whooping it up" and having a good time, he felt someone tap him on the shoulder and when he turned around "little Becky" was standing there and the first thing she said was, "So what's with the bag?" They had to talk loudly to compete with the music and Old Joe said, "This is where I keep all of my worthless opinions," to which she quickly responded, "Oh yeah? Well you probably should have thought about that a little sooner."

Then she gave him an elbow and playfully nudged him out of her way as she went around serving her other customers, while Old Joe stood there with a slight smile on his face and thought, *"Man, if I was only forty years younger."*

As much as Old Joe had loved The Roundhouse through the years, these two girls had made it even better, and he started wishing once again that he had more money to give each of them, but then he thought, *"Maybe it's for the best."* Because although his friendship with both of these girls had been totally innocent, Old Joe knew that word gets around and the last thing he wanted was for anyone's reputation to be sullied. *"When it's all said and done,"* he thought, *"all you have is your name."*

So he was listening to the music and enjoying the atmosphere while trying to savor every last moment that he could when "Sherri darlin'" suddenly ran by as if she were a quarterback and rather deftly handed off his beer. Then he gave her a twenty along with a high-five and after motioning for her to *"keep the change"* took a long steady drink from his cold Coors Light and for a brief moment started to miss "the good ol' days."

But then the music swept him up just like always and that old "Roundhouse magic" was suddenly there and he had his arms around people that he'd never met before as they were swaying back and forth and singing.

However, Old Joe still had his wits about him and was remembering what he came there to do so, even though he'd already drank more than he'd planned to, he was keeping a tight hold on his precious cargo.

Then somewhere around 6:30 he unzipped his old gray gym bag and took out the packages he'd brought for the girls, but while drinking his beer and waiting for them to come closer he thought, *"Fuck this already, I'm just gonna do it."*

Both girls happened to be near each other while they were waiting on different tables, so he called them together and after they all huddled-up as one in the simplest way possible he said, "Hey girls, I came into a little extra money the other day and I would like for both of you to have some, ok? So, here you go."

And as he gave them their brown paper packages, at exactly the same time and in exactly the same pitch they both said, "Aw Joe," and then they each said "thank you" and gave him a quick hug. "You're welcome ladies," replied the old man, "have a good evening." Then he casually turned toward the exit and walked out the door.

Just like Elvis, Old Joe had left the building.

62.

It was early evening with still plenty of daylight left, but Old Joe was feeling no pain. When he entered The Boathouse he was looking for only two things – Sarita and another beer.

Old Joe had always loved The Boathouse and he'd been going there for many years because of all of the things it offered – the music, the atmosphere, the beer, the women – but recently, he'd been going there mostly to see Sarita.

From the first time they met it was as if they had somehow known one another before, so even though it had only been a few months since their formal introduction, they had become very close. And it could no longer be said that it was simply the delusions of a lonely old man for the two of them actually seemed to be quite comfortable with each other, though neither one ever knew exactly what was going on inside the other one's head and at this juncture, it was anyone's guess.

But Old Joe couldn't find her when he first walked in, or a barstool, which seemed to be out of the question, so he leaned against the front wall before deciding once again to take the wide open seat on his now familiar wooden bench. Then after sitting there for a while he stretched out a little and thought, *You know, this ain't too awful bad,"* and he even had room for his old gym bag, which he had plopped down on the bench right next to him, and he was still smiling to himself when Sarita appeared.

She put her hand on his shoulder and said, "Hi Papa, how are you tonight?" And Old Joe said, "Oh, just fine my dear, and how are you?"

"To be honest Papa, I'm the one who's a little bit sleepy tonight, but stay right here and I'll bring you your beer." And then, as she was walking away, she turned half-way around and said, "I'll be right back."

And as Old Joe watched her make her way back to the bar he thought, *"What a sweetheart,"* and then began questioning himself yet again, *"Should I have left her more money?"* But then he applied the same rationale as he had before and told himself to start thinking about something else.

So he leaned back and began listening to the music; it was being performed on this evening by some male guitarist with one helluva good voice who Old Joe hadn't recalled ever hearing before. Then he closed his eyes.

And he must have nodded off for just a moment or two because the next thing he remembered was Sarita standing right above him saying, "Wake up now you old sleepy head," in the sweetest voice that he could possibly imagine. "Oh boy," he said, "who turned out the lights?" as Sarita reached down and handed him his beer. He turned the bottle around to see if the mountains were blue and then looked back at her with a smile and said, "Perfect."

Then he gave her a twenty and said, "Here you go honey, keep the change," to which Sarita responded, "Thanks Papa, and no more falling asleep now, ok?" and then she gave him that wonderful smile of hers along with a little wink before walking away.

And for the next few hours things went along quite nicely. He had an adequate seat, an ice cold beer, good entertainment, and he was receiving snippets of attention from a beautiful woman and he thought, *"What more could an old man ask for?"*

Furthermore, he finally decided that whatever this was that he had with Sarita, one thing was now certain – she trusted him. And likewise, he trusted her, and that made him feel good. Because to him, when you boiled it all down, life was just that simple – and so was that thing called love. And even though to a younger man this may have seemed foolish, to Old Joe it was as real as it could be.

But the place was getting more crowded, and Sarita was quite busy, so he decided that the time had come to move on. He opened his old gym bag and took out the brown package with the name "Sarita" neatly printed on the outside, and the only one that had masking tape on both the front and the back. Then, like a kid on prom night holding a corsage, he stood next to the bench and waited for her to walk over. And when she started moving his way he actually became a little nervous, but once she was there he summoned his courage and said, "Hey sweetie, I gotta go, but I wanted you to have this," then as he held out the package in his hand he continued, "you see, I recently came into ..." and before he could finish, or even say another word, Sarita came right up next to him and said, "Look Papa, I don't know what this is or why you're giving it to me, but thank you." Then, after graciously accepting her gift, she gave the old man a kiss on the cheek and softly whispered in his ear, "I love you Joe," and then she turned and walked away.

Old Joe was stunned.

He stood there and watched her leave.

But then, as she began to disappear back into the crowd, he quickly stepped onto the bench and after mustering up whatever strength his old body had left shouted at the top of his lungs, "Sarita!"

She heard the old man's voice and turned around. Then he yelled above the noise, "I love you too baby – with all my heart!" And for the briefest of moments, they looked at each other and smiled.

Then he jumped down from the bench, grabbed his old gym bag, put his right hand in the air to indicate "good-bye," and walked out.

Old Joe had left The Boathouse.

And Sarita.

63.

Old Joe's gym bag was almost empty.

There was only one package left to be delivered.

So while walking westward through Perry Park (and heading toward Mojito Bay) he was looking back on the day's events and was pretty satisfied with how things had gone up to this point. That is, with everything being considered. *"The best laid plans of mice and men,"* he thought, then laughed to himself when thinking about his earlier miscalculations at Frosty's.

But the more he thought about things, the more pleased he became, though mostly because he was nearer to the end than anything else, and for an instant he began to feel like he was young again – except for the fact that he was now an old man.

Yet, Old Joe was happy and he felt freer than he had in years.

Then he stopped for a moment and took a deep breath.

He looked all around.

As pretty as Put-In-Bay is in the daytime, the town comes alive on a summer's night, with the neon lights looking so beautiful and with the gentle breeze coming in from off the lake.

And then he took another deep breath.

He wanted to hold onto that moment for as long as he could, so he tried to let the air sink in – right down to his bones.

64.

It was a quarter 'til nine on another perfect summer evening as Old Joe was standing on the corner of Delaware and Catawba. He looked across the street at the Beer Barrel Saloon to see if "Big Sal" was working. *"He should probably be near the entrance checking ID's,"* he thought, but he couldn't locate him amongst all of the people.

So he crossed Catawba Avenue and stood at the entrance to Mojito Bay where he once again looked out upon a sea of people, before finally entering the grounds and feeling the sand give way with each step from underneath his feet. The Mojito was known for its rope swing chairs, but even though Old Joe had never much cared for them, it was still good to know that on nights like this Diago always kept that extra stool for him tucked away behind the bar.

"Hey Joe, how ya' doin' tonight?"

"Hey kid, what's new?"

"Oh, not too much – we're pretty busy as usual."

"Yeah, I can see that," said Old Joe, "it's like a can of sardines in here."

"Coors Light?" asked Diago, as he brought out the old man's barstool and sat it down in the sand, to which Old Joe replied, "That, my friend, would be delightful."

Then Diago walked over a few paces to the trough and pulled out an ice-cold bottle of suds, while Old Joe sat down with his beat-up gray gym bag and began thinking about how to deliver that last package. And even though he'd been drinking throughout the day, for the moment he was surprisingly coherent, and he was now as ready as ever to get rid of that bag along with the rest of his worldly possessions.

So when Diago came back a few seconds later and placed a cold bottle of Coors Light in front of him, he plopped that old gym bag down next to it on the bar and said, "Son, this is for you."

"For me? What is it?"

"It's a gift."

"Well, gee, that's awfully nice Old Joe, but I already have a gym bag at home."

"Not just the bag, you idiot, there's something inside – only, you can't open it until tomorrow."

"Tomorrow? Well that's only a couple hours away, so is it really going to make that much of a difference?"

"Uh, yeah, it'll make a difference – and I know what fucking time it is so can you please just do what I say?"

"All right Joe," said Diago, "let's review. This bag is for me, along with what's inside, but I can't open it until tomorrow – correct?"

"You got it."

"Ok – consider it done."

Then Old Joe stood up with his bottle of beer and guzzled the whole thing down in about four seconds.

"Impressive," said Diago.

"Old school," replied Old Joe, as he reached into his pocket and pulled out a ten dollar bill, then after putting it on the countertop he said, "Ok buddy, I'm outta here – have a good one."

And as they began to shake hands Diago asked, "Going so soon?"

"Yeah, there's a few things I gotta do – so I'll see ya' around."

"Ok," said Diago, "be safe."

Old Joe lowered his head slightly before looking back up and saying, "You know it kid."

But then, as he was walking away, he turned back toward Diago and said, "Hey kid, you stay good – you hear me? Or I'm gonna come back here and kick your ass!"

And with a smile Diago replied, "Always my father, always." Then the young bartender raised his voice above the crowd and added, "Hakuna matata," which made the old man smile and even chuckle a bit.

Then Old Joe turned back toward Catawba Avenue and continued on his way through the sand.

65.

After leaving Mojito Bay, Old Joe decided to make one last stop at Hooligan's.

He walked up to the bar and stood in between two empty chairs while waiting for the barkeep to come over.

Then he said, "I'll take a shot of whiskey."

"Ok, what's your flavor?" the man asked.

Old Joe looked at the bottles that were lined up against the mirror behind the bar – at all of the various sizes and shapes and colors – and after hesitating for a second he said, "You know, it really doesn't matter."

Then the barkeep poured him a shot and said, "That'll be five bucks even." So the old man reached into his pocket and pulled out a ten and said, "Here you go, keep the change."

To which the man replied, "Oh, ok, well thanks mister – much appreciated," and then he walked away. Old Joe stood there and looked at himself in the mirror. Then he reached into his pocket and pulled out the rest of his money.

For as long as he could remember, Old Joe had wanted to take his last breath and spend his last dime at the same time – at the very same moment if possible – and to leave nothing behind in this world.

So now, he was going to come as close as he possibly could.

In his right hand was all of the money he had left – a five, a ten, and a few singles, along with some loose change – and he laid it on the counter.

Then he drank his shot, put the empty glass down next to the money, and began walking toward the exit. When he got to the door, he looked back at the barkeep and raised his right hand as if to say "*good-bye*," and the man looked over and while raising his own right hand in recognition said, "Thanks again, have a good evening." Then Old Joe went outside.

He headed south on Catawba and began walking to his motel room.

And as he went along looking at the smiles on all of the pretty young faces that were walking the other way, it made him smile as well because, strangely enough, he felt happy, and content, and even a little warm on the inside, like the way he used to feel after drinking when *he* was young and didn't have a care in the world.

However, now it was time to focus.

He had to get on with what needed to be done.

66.

Old Joe entered his room and locked the door. He walked over to the refrigerator and grabbed a Coors Light. He opened the bottle, took a swig, and tossed the cap onto the floor. Then he kicked off his shoes and put them under the chair by his bed. He put his beer on the nightstand, took off his belt, rolled it up and sat it down on the chair.

And then he did something that he hadn't done in years.

He knelt down next to his bed, made the sign of the cross, and began to pray. He said one Our Father, one Hail Mary, and a prayer that he remembered from childhood:

"Now I lay me down to sleep, I pray the Lord my soul to keep, if I should die before I wake, I pray the Lord my soul to take. Amen"

And then he added, *"Please take me Lord – please take this sinner."*

Then he got up and sat on the bed. He pulled open the small table drawer that was next to him and took out two bottles of sleeping pills that he'd purchased months before and emptied them onto the nightstand.

Then he took out his other medications and began spilling them out as well. One by one, he sat there emptying the small plastic bottles and then tossing them across the room. He liked listening to the hollow sound they made as they bounced off of the ceramic tiles near the bathroom.

To Old Joe, it was the sound of nothing.

He repeated this process until all of the pills were lying on top of the nightstand. Then he looked down and noticed that the sleeping pills were white whereas the other pills had different colors.

There were reds, and yellows, and blues.

Then he grabbed a handful of sleeping pills, put them in his mouth, and washed them down with his beer. Then he grabbed another handful, and another, and washed them down until all of the white was gone.

He finished the rest of his beer and put the empty bottle on the nightstand.

Then as he looked down at the remaining colors, at all of those reds and yellows and blues, he thought, *"How beautiful – just like the neon lights at Put-In-Bay."*

Then he laid himself down, closed his eyes, and went to sleep.

67.

When we finally met, Old Joe was surrounded by light.

He was in a place that has no space or time – and though he hadn't as yet been accepted into heaven, Our Lord had indeed taken him.

So, after explaining how I'd been with him throughout his entire life, I gave him his assignment, or his penance if you will, just as my assignment had been given to me – to watch over the living.

But, rather than a single person, he was entrusted with a place.

It's a place he knew well.

A place close to heaven.

He remains there to this day.

Song Lyrics

Across the Field; William A. Dougherty, Jr. (1915)

Buckeye Battle Cry; Frank Crumit (1919)

(Works first registered or published in the United States before 1926 are in the public domain and free of copyright.)